THE
BLENDER

A YOUNG LADY'S JOURNEY
OF
PAIN, REVELATION, AND TRIUMPH

Written By
Ebony Maddrey MS

THE BLENDER

ISBN: 978-1-312-51031-9
Copyright © 2014
THE BLENDER
A YOUNG LADY'S JOURNEY OF PAIN, REVELATION, AND TRIUMPH
Ebony Maddrey MS
Editing: Ebony Maddrey MS
Cover Graphics: Patchwork Designs
Printed in the United States
All Rights Reserved

Dedication

This book is dedicated to all of the young women out there who have no way of understanding the internal conflict of being continuously hurt or disappointed. It is my hope that you find peace in your story and share with others with the expectation that they are able to find healing too.

Acknowledgements

I would like to start by thanking God who is the creator of all things. He has truly blessed me in many areas and with gifts that I can use to reach out to others. I would like to acknowledge my family and friends for all of their patience with me and in pushing me to get through this piece. I appreciate all of you.

Particularly my mother for displaying what it truly means to: *press on in spite of what things look like.* I know that you don't say it often, but I know that you love deeper than words could ever express.

To my father who is no longer here, I take away all of the lessons learned by both your absence and your presence. I feel your spirit often when I go about my daily routines. I will forever, be appreciative of all of the young people that I have worked with over the years for aiding in molding me into the therapist that I have become. All of our experiences together are priceless. I am grateful for all of those painful experiences that I have encountered because they have truly pushed me into a more humble, wise, and transparent woman. Those experiences alone have enabled me to connect to my audience on an entirely different level.

I would like to give a special shout out to everyone who held me accountable. You did just what I asked of all of you and now I have another finished piece. You were absolutely right. *The youth have been waiting on me.* I am not sure where this journey will lead me I just pray that my steps are continuously ordered in the word.

I will forever be grateful for meeting Mrs. Sharon Bryant. She has always led by example and continues to touch the lives of the youth just as she touched mines over 15 years ago. Thank you for being a beacon of light.

To my children, I know that it isn't always easy to put up with my ranting. Know that I love you more than life itself and that I want you all to succeed on a supernatural level. Proverbs 3:5-6 *Lean not to your own understanding and acknowledge Him in all of your ways.* Keep this is mind and you will always persevere.

THE

BLENDER

Foreword

In 1991, while working as a Crisis Intervention Counselor, in the largest high school in the state of Delaware, I had the privilege of meeting the remarkable author of this book! A quick-witted, petite young woman, Ebony Maddrey appeared innocent, but at the same time, mature beyond her years. With her keen intellect, and sometimes piercing ability to communicate, Ebony could contend with anyone in a verbal dispute or otherwise. Her very distinctive eyes would sometimes reflect her feelings and/or her mood. It became very obvious to me that Ebony was a bright, perceptive young woman, but guarded in her approach to other people and circumstances outside of her familiar circle. Herself a leader, in a close-knit cadre of devoted friends, neighbors, and cousins, Ebony had a mind of her own...often times, it seemed that she was the "voice of reason" among her peer group.

Growing up in a small, working class, African-American community, located on the outskirts of Wilmington, Delaware, Ebony realized her calling and passion to help others who were hurting and in need of support. As her dreams continue to materialize, I am in eager anticipation of things to come! One of Ebony's ultimate objectives is to meet the highly celebrated Oprah Winfrey. I would not be surprised if this happened sooner than later. Her sincere passion to help other young people who are struggling with the difficult but obscure realities of life has led to the writing of this book…a manual created to promote greater understanding and hopefully, less stereotypical characterization of our children, who are in crisis. I most admire Ebony for actualizing her ideals and her passion with this book, and trust that its contents will make a difference in the lives of many.

Very sincerely,

Sharon Bryant, M.Ed.
Secondary School Counselor

Preface

In the tenth grade I finally realized that I had a passion to help others and to set an example for those who came behind me. My dreams of becoming an engineer or a doctor where becoming more and more distant. I longed to have the same effect that my counselor had on me with other children. I wanted them to know that in spite of the trials that they may encounter in life, there is always light at the end of the tunnel. It wasn't until I was older that I understood that not only was this lady a counselor, but her title was the Family Crisis Therapist. I had no idea that she was housed in the school to help children like me realize the importance of being accountable and working through the root causes of various problems. Although I wasn't in a crisis, so I thought, subliminally I was a walking crisis.

Completely unaware of the ability that I carried to self-destruct at any given moment.

It is with a great appreciation of her direct impact on me as a young girl that I dove into the world of counseling and my hunger to help others was ignited. I created the character of Bianca James to depict the typical life of a teenaged girl and how her deep rooted anger caused her to be labeled as a misfit who was destined for failure. All it took was for one individual to take an interest and to believe that she was capable of succeeding without focusing on where and what she had come from. Many young girls will be able to relate to this triumphant young lady and will see pieces of themselves or pieces of their peers in Bianca's character.

EBONY MADDREY MS

Table of Contents

TRIUMPH

Prelude

Flashback

****

The room was dark and damp. There was a queen sized bed and a cot on the side. The cot was next to the window. So there was very little room to maneuver between the bed and the cot. GiGi slept on one side of the bed and He slept on the other which just so happened to be closest to the cot. There were two of us on the cot. I can remember being cold as I slept. Reaching for the covers in the dark but unable to find them; I balled up in a fetal position to shield myself from the shiver.

Bianca was awakened as she realized that something had slid into her panties. She laid there as she felt fingers crawling across her underdeveloped, six year old, hairless vagina. It was cold in the dark room where at least four other people were sleeping. There were adults in the living room. Bianca knew that her mother was out there but was afraid to scream. She feared waking everyone in the house. He continued to fondle her private area. Bianca was unable to move as she drifted away mentally. Minutes went by for what seemed like hours. Bianca wet herself.

He snatched his hands from her panties and quietly whispered "shhhhhhh."

Bianca jumped up out of the wetness and off of the cot and fumbled to make her way to the door of the small bedroom. Heart racing. She was able to find a pair of pants on top of the hamper. Bianca didn't know whose pants she grabbed or if they were adult pants there was just a sliver of light that peered through the crack of the door. Bianca stepped out of her wet panties and quietly opened the door to the bedroom. She stood in the hallway half naked as she stepped into a pair of pants that were a size too small for her. They must belong to one of the cousins.

Bianca went into the dark living room where her mother and her aunt were sleeping on two separate couches. They had just come in from hanging out not long ago. Bianca unable to process what had just taken place stood there on the side of her sleeping mother, wearing two small pants that she just so happened to put on backwards, crying silently on the outside but screaming loudly on the inside.

Bianca stood there with a blank and distant stare, body stiffened, afraid to wake anyone, and afraid to go to sleep; she stood there in the dark until the sun began to beam through the window shades.

PAIN

Fighting For My Right

"There she goes again, fighting on the other students and lashing out towards authority figures," the two teachers in the hall proclaimed as they walked past the classroom where the explosive young girl was tossing around desks and chairs.

"No one is going to tell me what to do! I can do whatever the hell I feel like doing!" Bianca yelled as the guards were sent to restrain her. "These niggas are going to learn how to show a chick some respect around here!"

"Bianca! Calm down so that we can let you go!" exclaimed the male guard.

"Calm down? Nigga you calm down! Let go of me!"
Bianca continued to scream and wrestle with the guards
until she grew tired.

After screaming, crying, and fighting Bianca caught a
terrible headache. She continued to sob as she mumbled,
"I'm tired of being disrespected... I'm so tired of being
disrespected." The guards walked on each side of Bianca as
they escorted her to the ISS (In School Suspension) room.
The Dean of Discipline was already waiting for her after
receiving the call about the blow up in class.

Mrs. Bryant, the school counselor, came into the room
where Bianca was being held and began to talk with her.
"Bianca," said Mrs. Bryant, "you cannot continue to go
around here beating on the other students and destroying
property."

"He shouldn't have grabbed my butt!" yelled
Bianca. "He's lucky that I only hit him with the chair."
Bianca rolled her eyes and crossed her arms as she slumped
down in the desk she was sitting in.

Mrs. Bryant informed Bianca that after speaking
with the Dean of Discipline that this episode resulted in a

three day suspension and community service for the destruction of property.

BUS

The bus ride home was just as hectic as the school day. The kids were jumping across seats, smoking weed, and making out. Bianca stared out the window watching the tree lined streets and the rundown houses. Kenny, one of the best basketball players in the school plopped down in the seat next to Bianca.

"What's up "B"?" he said, as he smiled at her with his perfect teeth. "I heard that you had to handle your business with that jerk, Melvin today."

"Yeah, I had to let him know that he was messing with the wrong chick. I bet he'll think twice before trying to grab someone else's ass again."

"Hell yeah he will!" Kenny smirked. "Oh snap, can I use your phone for a second?" Kenny asked as he patted his pockets. "I need to call my mom to tell her that I'm playing ball this afternoon."

Bianca handed Kenny her phone and gave him a semi smile before resuming her position of staring out of the window. She was actually thinking of all of the yelling that her mother was going to do as soon as she walked in the house. Kenny handed Bianca her phone as he grabbed his book bag and prepared to get off at the next stop. "Thanks B," he said as he stood and walked up the aisle of the bus.

HOME

"Damn, Bianca Renee! I send you to school for you to get a good education. Not for you to go the hell in there and act like you're bionic woman or the wife of Rambo. I am so sick of you being suspended every other week. You know better Bianca and you better start acting like it or I am going to ship your ass off somewhere, where the kids are really tough and half ass crazy!"

"Whatever mom, maybe I'll be better off somewhere else anyhow." Bianca stormed off and went into her bedroom.

She slammed the door and began to listen to her Keyshia Cole CD. The words played loudly through the speakers.

"I'm trying to be happy...

I'm just like you...

look in the mirror and what do you see"

As the song began to permeate her thoughts, Bianca fell asleep.

(FLASHBACK)

It was dark in the room and everything was still. Fingers began to walk across her hairless and undeveloped vagina. Massaging the area between her legs that had never been touched, an

*uncontrollable sensation came over her and she
wet the bed.*

Bianca jumped up in a cold sweat to find that she had
just peed on herself. She took the sheets off of the bed,
undressed from the wet clothes that were sticking to her
body and threw everything in a pile on the floor. Bianca
went into the bathroom and turned the shower on full blast.
While in the shower, she cried silently to herself as she
remembered the episode vividly of her grandmother's
boyfriend fondling her as a five year old girl.

After her shower, Bianca took her pile of wet clothing
and bedding down to the basement and put them into the
washer. She went into the kitchen to find that her mother
had left a plate in the microwave. As she sat and devoured
the plate of chicken, mashed potatoes, and string beans,
Bianca began to internalize the comments that her mother
had made earlier.

"Would she really send me away? Why can't I stop
getting into so much trouble all of the time? Would my
mom really be better off if I weren't around?" It was one

question after another and Bianca began to feel overwhelmed.

This is ridiculous, she said to herself as she began to run dishwater to wash off the dishes. As her hands swished around in the sudsy water Bianca began to talk to herself. Shit, I have to be tough. Shoot, if I don't look out for B", who else will? Who protected me from them nasty ass fuckers when I was younger? Right, nobody! I can still get a good education. I know that's why she moved into this district. I'll get a good education while protecting myself as well. Like I said, no one is going to disrespect me again. Not now. Not ever. Bianca smiled as she cleaned off the counter and continued with her self-talk. She found herself smiling at the thought of always being in control.

Ring....ring...ring....

Bianca looked around for her cell phone as its ring tone chimed thinking, who could possibly be calling her now?

"Hello?"

"Hey „B" what are you doing?"

"Who is this?"

"Girl, stop playing."

"No, seriously, who is this?" The
voice on the other end paused.

Kenny laughed and responded, "It's Kenny, the best looking dude that you'll ever come across."

Bianca laughed. "I don't recall giving you my number."
"That's because you didn't," Kenny said. "You just gave me your phone."
Bianca sat there for a minute. "Boy you are CRAZY! I thought you needed to call your mom."

Kenny said, "Well, I did call my mom, but only to snag your number."
"You could have asked for it silly," Bianca replied.
"Please, after what you did to Melvin's whack behind? Imagine me asking you for your number. You probably would have sucker punched me with some brass knuckles or something."
"Well, you do know that my alias is Mrs. Rambo," Bianca said. By now both Bianca and Kenny were smiling uncontrollably on opposite ends of the telephone.

"Well, „B" it has gotten really late and I truly enjoyed busting it up with you. However, it is almost two in the

morning and I have to get some rest or it will interfere with my good looks."

"Yeah, I'll just enjoy my little vacation, I suppose."

"How long are you suspended for?"

"Three days."

"What are you going to do to occupy your time?"

"Read."

"Be for real. You're going to read while you are out on suspension?"

"Yup, believe it or not; I actually enjoy reading. I have a few books lying around here on Alfred Binet"

"Alfred who?" Kenny replied.

"Binet, he was known for creating the first intelligence test." "Wow, look at you Miss B, interested in the mind huh?"

"Yes, I've always had this strange curiosity about how the mind works and why people do half of the things that they do. One day, I'll schedule you for an appointment to sit on my couch and work through your issues," Bianca teased. Kenny laughed and said, "Well it was good talking to you. Have a good night „B"."

"Thanks, Kenny you do the same."

Over the next couple of days, Bianca was able to get through the books that she had on Binet. She also utilized her

time to strategize different ways of doing a better job of staying focused and out of trouble. On the day that she returned to school there was a message waiting for her in homeroom class.

SCHOOL

"Bianca, Mrs. Bryant needs for you to report to her office at 10 o'clock." Mr. Hamm informed her.

"For what?" Bianca asked.

"I'm not sure." Mr. Hamn declared, "I am just relaying the message so make sure that you get there."

After second period Bianca headed for the 2nd floor hallway that housed Mrs. Bryant's office. It was small for an office but had just enough space for two chairs, a desk, and a bookshelf. There were a few pictures here and there, a poem or some sort of inspirational piece on the wall, and a plant. There was something about the atmosphere of the room that caused Bianca to relax.

Mrs. Bryant was dressed in a one piece navy blue dress from Talbot's that flared out at the bottom with a belt that wrapped around her waist. She wore a strand of pearls around her neck along with some pearl studs. She was tall and confident in her demeanor with a complexion that resembled the color of freshly ground cocoa. She appeared to be a highly intelligent and pleasant woman. Her temperament was easy going and extremely nurturing.

"Hello Bianca, come in and have a seat," Mrs. Bryant stated as she smiled and extended her arm in the direction of the seat closest to her desk. Bianca sat as she greeted Mrs. Bryant with a smile in return.

"Well, were you able to do some reflecting during your time off of school?"

"Yes, and I admit that I am tired of getting into trouble as well. I came up with a plan and a commitment for myself to work harder at doing the right thing, consider the people around me, and how my actions affect them too."

"Oh, you must have had a heart to heart with your mother," Mrs. Bryant stated.

"That too," Bianca replied, "and she is really getting frustrated with me and my behaviors. I just want to be able

to come to school, learn and do what I need to do in order to get out of here."

Mrs. Bryant sat patiently as Bianca continued to express herself.

"I want to come to school without having to fight and feel that I have to defend myself all the time."

Once Bianca, had finished completely, Mrs. Bryant stated "You do know that you determine your own future Bianca James and you are the only one who can control which route you wish to take in life. It is all about self-control. Bianca, you have special gifts and talents and if you don't come to understand that very quickly, you can ruin your entire future."

Bianca sat there taking it all in and Mrs. Bryant could see that she struck a nerve. "Well, sweetie that's just some food for thought. Let's get to the reason that you are here. I called you in to discuss the community service portion of your suspension. I have arranged for you to report to a good friend of mine, her name is Ms. Mary, Mary Washington." Mrs. Bryant scribbled something on her notepad. "Here is the address that you are to report to, she will be waiting for you on Saturday at 10:30."

"What will I have to do?" Bianca questioned.

"You'll see, just make sure that you are dressed comfortably and that you have on comfortable shoes. This is mandatory Bianca and I have already informed your mother of your responsibility to show up for this project." Mrs.

Bryant declared.

"Alright Mrs. Bryant, I'll do it, but only because the lady is your friend."

As Mrs. Bryant wrote out Bianca's pass to return to class, Bianca stood up putting the address in her pocket and gathered her things. "Remember what I said Bianca, you determine your own future."

Bianca left the office and headed towards her third period class. On the way she wondered about what type of arrangement Mrs. Bryant had made for her. What if I have to clean out porta-potties or pick up trash on the highway? Oh, my goodness!!!!! "I am going to be so embarrassed!" Bianca shouted.

Upon entering the Algebra II class, Bianca noticed that Melvin was smirking at her. She started to say something totally inappropriate to him but thought better of it and

smiled at him saying, "How are you today Melvin?" as she walked past his desk.

Melvin sat there dumbfounded and didn't know how to take her remarks. Bianca made her way to her seat and began to take down the notes that were up on the whiteboard. She worked diligently at completing the assigned tasks as not to fall behind in her work for today. The bell rang and the halls were flooded with students coming from all angles of the school.

"Yo B welcome back baby!" she heard a voice say as she began to switch the books in her locker with the ones she would need for her afternoon classes.

Bianca looked around and saw that it was Kenny who gave her the shout out. When she spotted him, he began grinning real hard as he approached her.

"Hey young boy what's up?" Bianca said as Kenny invaded her space.

"Nothing really, I wanted to know if you wanted to hang out this weekend and catch that new movie on Saturday?"

"Well, I have to see if my mom will budge on letting me off of punishment. I also have to do this community service thing on Saturday and I don't know how long it's going to be."

"Damn „B", community service huh?" Kenny said as he looked her over.

"Yup," she replied.

"Well you let me know and we'll work it out from there. I'll call you later," Kenny said as he ran to make it to his fourth period class before the late bell rang. Bianca finished with her books and headed towards the lunch room.

During lunch Bianca sat with her usual crew; Tiara, Shantelle, and Veronica.
Tiara, the loudest one out of the group exclaimed, "Girl you are so lucky that you got to take a few days off from having to get up early and come in this place!"

"Not really," stated Bianca, "I had several things to do and would have preferred to be sitting in class completing my assignments and hanging out with" my girls." "You are so whack!" Veronica said.

"No, you are whack! My mom had a whole list of chores for me to do and the list had to be done by the time she got home from work, every day. Eight hours of housework for three days. Straight torture," Bianca stated. Veronica laughed, "You're right that is torture! I think that

I would have preferred to be in school too, my whack friend." They all laughed in unison.

"Yeah, I'm glad that you all are laughing," Bianca said as she tried to make a straight face. "I still have to make up three days' worth of missed work."

They all finished up at the lunch table and headed their separate ways into the hallway. At the end of the school day they all gathered around the common area in front of the school. Shantelle, the one who always kept a boyfriend stood all starry eyed as she waited for Devin, her current boo, to come and walk her to the bus.

Tiara and Veronica clowned her every chance that they got. "Look at this hussy! What, you don't know how to get to your bus?" the two of them mocked.

"Shut up y'all! It's not about that and y'all know it. Just shut up!" Shantelle scowled at them.

"Yo BJ, check out Shantelle, her latest project is Devin Williamson from the east side."

Bianca yelled back at them, "Leave her alone. Y'all know that y'all want to get with a few of his boys!"

Veronica and Tiara looked at Bianca as if she were talking in some unknown language. Truth be told, they both had the hot's for Devin's closest friends.

"Girl hush, you swear you know everything!" Tiara proclaimed as she rolled her eyes at Bianca.

"Hey Devin, how was your day today?" Shantelle asked as he took her backpack and headed towards her bus.

"It was alright, how about yours babe?"

"Well, since you asked, I have two projects due in science and I am really excited that we are going to begin dissecting animals next week..."

EBONY MADDREY MS

So let's not get tired of doing what is good.

At just the right time we will reap a harvest of blessing if we

don't give up. ~Galatians 6:9

Community Service

Early Saturday morning…

"Get up Bianca!" yelled her mother. "Get up and get dressed so that you can go and do this damn community service."

"Dang, Ma, its 8:30 and I don't have to be there until 10:30," Bianca said as she covered her head with her polk-a-dot comforter.

"Well too bad. I am not going to be rushing around trying to get you somewhere at the last minute!" her mother exclaimed.

Bianca got up and stomped into the bathroom. "Dang, she makes me sick!" Bianca said under her breath. "What did you say?" Her mother yelled from the hallway. "How in the hell does somebody make you sick BJ, when you keep running around fighting on every damn body? You make me sick! Wasting my time on a Saturday morning, now hush up and get dressed damn it!"

Bianca got into the shower and had the water on full blast. She thought about the events leading up to her having to do community service as the water beat down on her back. Why am I always so angry? Why did they have to feel on me? What ever happened to just being a happy go lucky kid? Filthy ass bastards! Tears began to well up in Bianca's eyes. She put her head under the water and began to sing to her herself. *"I asked for a sign from the sweat Lord above. I know the answer is inside of me, but when you think you're in love, you only see what you want to see. All I see is you for me and me for you. All I really want is to be happy..."* Bianca began to lather herself as she continued to sing her own rendition of Mary J. Blige"s song "Happy".

By the time she got out of the shower her mother had already had breakfast ready. Bianca, dressed quickly in a Hollister jogging suit, pulled her hair back into a low ponytail, and put on a baseball cap. She went into the dining room and sat at the table with her mother. The two of them ate in silence and then headed out the door.

Bianca and her mother pulled up in front of a big white building that had blue letters across the front that read: *The Children's Home*, Bianca turned to her mother and asked, "What do they do here?"

"I have no idea Bianca, you should have asked Mrs. Bryant," her mother replied. They got out of the car and walked towards the entrance of the building. Once inside, Bianca noticed the beautiful décor of the place. Everything on the inside was blue and white and gave of the aura of being by the ocean. The receptionist came out and asked how she could assist them. Bianca stated that she had an appointment with Ms. Mary Washington.

Ms. Washington came from the back. She was a small petite woman with gray hair. She greeted Bianca and her mother and invited them into her office. Upon entering her office, Bianca noticed pictures of children, awards, and newspaper articles hanging on the walls and sitting on the shelves. Ms. Washington sat behind her large oak desk and

began to inform Bianca and her mother of the mission of *The Children's Home.*

"*The Children's Home* houses children who are runaways, victims of abuse and neglect, and who are orphans of the state." Bianca was anxious on the inside and wanted to know more about the kids in the program. She wanted to see them and to talk to them about their experiences. Bianca began to think back on some of her own experiences of being touched on as a little girl; thoughts that her mother was completely oblivious too. When she began to feel the emotions beginning to boil on the inside she quickly redirected her thoughts and ignorantly asked, "Well enough about that Ms. Washington, what exactly is it that you want me to do?"

Her mother looked at her awkwardly and yelled, "Bianca Renee" James you better check that attitude of yours and show Ms. Washington some respect!"

Ms. Washington looked over her glasses and exclaimed to Bianca's mother, "She will be fine you can come back to get her at 4:30."

"4:30!" Bianca screamed. "You mean to tell be that I'll be her for six hours? What can I possibly do here for six hours?"

Bianca's mother excused herself and smiled at Bianca as she walked out of the office waving her hand,

"I'll see you at 4:30 pumpkin".

Well, Miss Bianca, Mrs. Bryant has told me a little bit about you. So…. You've been having a few run-ins with people at the school huh?"

"You can say so," Bianca said as she got up and began to examine the awards and news articles posted throughout the room. "Ms. Washington, what am I going to do here today?" Bianca asked in a more polite way.

"For starters, Bianca we are going to do some yard work around the grounds."

"Yard work?" Bianca laughed and said with a slight attitude, "I am sorry but I do not do yard work."

"Today you do," said Ms. Washington, "now follow me."

Ms. Washington led Bianca into a beautiful courtyard filled with exotic flowers and funny looking trees.
There were white flowers, purple flowers, and orange flowers.
There were pink, yellow, white, and red roses. Bianca saw trees that were shaped funny and trees that had leaves shaped like

butterflies. There were birds as big as the pigeons back in the city, but instead of being black or gray, they were white. There were birds that were blue like the sky and birds that were red like apples. The courtyard was so pretty that it reminded Bianca of a scene from a movie.

Bianca looked at Ms. Washington and said, "There is nothing that needs to be done in this garden."

Ms. Washington Calmly responded by saying, "There is a lot to do Bianca."

As they walked deeper into the garden, Bianca began to hear voices. Once they reached their destination Bianca stood in total amazement. There was huge wall with all sorts of pictures and sayings on it. There were tables covered with all sorts of art supplies. There were also children of different ages sitting around in a circle talking amongst themselves. Bianca noticed that there were two empty chairs in the circle. Ms. Washington greeted the group and introduced Bianca. They all responded in unison, "Welcome Bianca!" Bianca sarcastically returned their greeting by waving her hand and saying, "Hello."

Ms. Washington took her seat and patted the chair next to her signaling for Bianca to sit next to her. As Bianca looked around at the faces of each individual in the group, she couldn't help but wonder if they were there doing community service or if they were residents of *The Children's Home.* Her mind began to wonder in several different directions. "Focus B," she told herself, "just stay focused." Ms. Washington sat with her hands folded in her lap and again welcomed the group. She proceeded to give instructions on what would be done for the remainder of their time together.

The instructions were for each person in the group to pull a ribbon out of the basket that was sitting on the ground in the middle of the circle. Each person had to name something or someone that has hurt them in the past. Then we were instructed to state whether we have forgiven ourselves or the person for that particular hurt or pain. When the person to the right takes their turn they have to tie their ribbon to that person until everyone's ribbon is connected to someone else's. Bianca sat there and thought to herself,

What in the world did Mrs. Bryant sign me up for? This is

not what you call cleaning up the street nor is it cleaning up the garden.

Ms. Washington began, "When I was a young girl, my father left my mother for another woman and never came back; I have finally forgiven him."

The boy on the right of Ms. Washington went next. He said, "Two years ago my mother's boyfriend stabbed my mother 26 times in front of me and my brother. Now I have a really hard time sleeping because I am always worried about her; I have not forgiven him. The boy tied his ribbon to Ms. Washington's ribbon.

The next person went and said, "My cousin's boyfriend crept into my room when she was at work and did really horrible things to me; I have not forgiven him." She tied her ribbon to the boy who went after Ms. Washington. Bianca continued to sit there thinking, why would Mrs. Bryant send me to a place like this? I never told her about anything that has ever happened to me.

The next person went, she talked about how her mother was a drug addict and Children and Youth Services had to remove her and her siblings from their home. She admitted that she has finally forgiven her mother. She tied her ribbon to the person that spoke before her.

Bianca began to reflect on all the times her cousin and her grandmother's boyfriend took advantage of her.
Bianca's thoughts ran rampantly through her mind. Her chest began to heave up and down and she began to get all hot on the inside as the anger began to rise up in her. A tear ran down Bianca's cheek as she sat and listened to one story after another. She watched as the ribbons were tied together. She watched as some of the others in the circle had tears running down their faces also. She watched as Ms.
Robinson offered a comforting nod as each person spoke.

Bianca suddenly realized that her turn would be up after two more people. She became extremely uncomfortable and began to fiddle with the string in her hand. Oh my god, what am I going to do? I have never told anyone about these incidents. What will they think? Will it get back to my mom? Should I make up a story instead of telling the truth? Bianca's stream of tears became more fluid. She sat there as she listened to the story of the boy sitting next to her.

"My brother always called me ugly and I always felt like I was different. No matter how hard I tried to be close to my brother he always found a way to put me down and to make me feel like I wasn't worth anything. I would have never tried to commit suicide if it weren't for him tormenting me; I am still working on forgiving him." The boy tied his ribbon to the girl sitting next to him.

The group looked at Bianca as she sat there sobbing silently; waiting for her to begin to disclose some sort of hurtful situation. None of the other kids had faces at this point they all appeared to be images of different colors without any definition. Bianca felt a lump well up in her throat and although in her mind she was sharing her story, her mouth wasn't moving. Bianca threw the ribbon down on the ground and ran away from the circle.

She ran past the beautifully colored flowers, and past the fountains, and past the odd looking trees. Bianca stopped as she got closer to the entry way of the building realizing that her mother would not be back for several hours. She had no idea as to where this building was exactly located and had no money to catch the bus even if she wanted to.

Bianca turned around now with the building behind her and the garden in front of her. She stood there thinking about all of the stories that were shared within the circle and how she had responded. Why did I just run off like that? If everyone else was able to share then why couldn't I?

Bianca began to slowly walk back into the garden. She came across a bench and decided to sit there because she was embarrassed to face the group. Bianca sat on the bench and observed the scenery. She leaned back on the bench so that she could look up at the clouds in the sky. Bianca heard someone walking towards her but she continued to look at the clouds. As the person got closer, Bianca realized that it was one of the girls from the group. She sat down next to Bianca on the bench and leaned back as well.

"My name is Simone," the girl said as she pointed to a cloud that she said looked like a whale. They both laughed briefly. "So, Bianca why did you run off like that?" Simone asked.

"To be honest with you, sitting there listening to everyone's stories brought back a lot of hurtful memories, things that I have tried to forget about."

Bianca's eyes welled up with tears and although she was embarrassed she felt a slight sense of relief. Simone sat with Bianca in silence. She told Bianca that the only way to heal is to give those feelings that she tried to forget about a voice. Simone sat a while longer and then eventually said, "Well, I have to get back to the others." She wrote her number down on a receipt that she had in her pocket and told Bianca to give her a call anytime if and when she ever wanted to talk. Simone got up and disappeared into the back of the garden. Bianca sat on the bench a bit longer before deciding to rejoin the group.

Once back in the group Bianca subconsciously heard Simone saying over and over again „the only way to heal is to give those feelings a voice". Bianca began to feel encouraged and she eventually shared a piece of her story that came from the pit of her stomach and the confines of her remembrance....

"I remember staying over at my Grandmother's house," Bianca began. "I slept in the room on a cot next to my Grandmother's bed. The room was damp and dark. As I slept I felt something crawling across my private parts and into my panties. I remember feeling like I was dreaming until I wet the bed. I was so afraid that I fumbled to find some clothes and sat in the living room for the rest of the night, scared to close my eyes. I didn't understand what had happened until it happened again."

Bianca was surprised at her ability to share this experience that she had never shared before. She was overwhelmed with feelings of anxiety, anger, and relief all at the same time. With a stream of tears going down her face, Bianca tied her ribbon on to the others.

SCHOOL

Monday morning instead of going to homeroom, Bianca marched straight to Mrs. Bryant's office. Mrs. Bryant was not in the office when she arrived. Bianca sat and waited patiently. Thoughts flooding her head, Is there something that Mrs. Bryant knows? Is there something that I did? My mom doesn't even know, why in the world would she send me to do community service at that facility?

As the first bell rang the halls became flooded with familiar voices. One in particular was the voice of Kenny.

"Hey B, I called you several times this weekend and you never got back with me."

"Yeah, I'm truly sorry, my weekend was overwhelming and I didn't do much talking to anyone so please don't take it personal."

Just then Mrs. Bryant entered into the suite where her office was located.

"Kenny I'll get with you later, I really need to speak with Mrs. Bryant."

"Cool", Kenny said as he turned and walked away and headed to his homeroom class.

"Mrs. Bryant why did you send me there?" Bianca questioned.

"I sent you there so that you could get a sense of what other people go through and for you to understand that you are not alone Bianca. You have to give the pain that you have on the inside a voice. Give it a voice so that other people can understand you and why you respond to things the way that you do."

"But Mrs. Bryant," Bianca interrupted, "What makes you think that I am in pain? I'm not in any pain. I just don't like people telling me what to do or trying to get over on me."

"Bianca dear," she replied, " I know that you are in pain and you simply try to cover it up by fighting and cursing people out all of the time."

Bianca's eyes began to swell up with tears. She sat there trying to figure out how this woman was able to read her so easily.

Mrs. Bryant noticed that Bianca was desperately trying to fight back the tears that were trying to burst through. She calmly looked over at Bianca and said, "Start at the beginning."

"What do you mean?" Bianca asked as the salty tears began to fall down her face and slide over her lips.

"I mean, start from the first traumatic event that you can recall."

Bianca's mind began to race. Do I tell her about the nasty ass guy who fondled me when I was younger? Do I tell her about being scared when my aunt passed away? Do I tell her about my first sexual encounter? The list went on and on. Bianca knew that she didn't want Mrs. Bryant to judge her or to think less of her so she vouched to go with something that she never talked about. Something that was completely out of her control, something that she was certain had affected other people, and something that she wanted help with understanding.

"Ok." Bianca took a deep breath and began to share her recollection of the night that one of her favorite Aunts passed away.

Challenged by the hype of the MJ dance challenge; I hit the high score going against my cousin. Everyone laughed as we imitated none other than the greatest performer of all time (Michael Jackson). Tired and sweaty, I passed the controller over to Ava who was next in line.

I walked into the kitchen to get a cup of the virgin daiquiri that Auntie had made. That was our thing with her. She would make them just like she did for her adult gatherings minus the alcohol. I so wanted to see what the Bacardi would taste like added to my cup but knew that she would never go for it. I sat and rubbed my hands over the smooth tinted bottle of Bacardi that was visible thinking of the day that I would finally get to taste it. I couldn't wait for the day that I would get to sample a daiquiri with ALL of the key ingredients in it. I grabbed a cup and Auntie poured the virgin version of her signature drink into a cup for me. How refreshing; I thought as I sucked on pieces of ice wrapped in strawberry bits.

"Auntie you're the best I told her. Only you would allow us to have a sleepover on a school night." She looked at me and smiled as she continued to flour up the chicken pieces that she was frying up for our dinner. I stood there staring at her feeling like; I want to be like her when I grow up; even mannered, independent, and stable. I couldn't recall ever seeing my Auntie upset; just the one time when we decided to walk home from the skating rink. She was upset because she was worried about us. I think it hurt her more to discipline my cousin than it hurt my cousin to receive one of her only butt whooping's.

When she noticed that I was still standing there. She turned to me and inquired about my day and how school was going thus far.

"Everything is fine, Auntie, I am not having any issues in school right now. I haven't been in ISS (In School Suspension) for the past week."

"Wow BJ," she stated, "that's progress. Keep it up and let's hope that for the remainder of the year you'll be able to stay out of there. You are too smart to keep getting into trouble. Why don't you work on giving those teachers something else to talk about? It will also be a good break for your mom. Bianca you do know that she gets really stressed out when she receives those phone calls from the principal and when she has to leave work to come and get you. Bianca it's embarrassing not only to us but you should be embarrassed as well. You need to see yourself for the Queen that you are. Your attitude doesn't line up with the beauty you possess."

I sat there as Auntie calmly lectured me. Everything that she said was true. I just didn't know how to control myself once someone made me mad.

I wanted to please my mother. I didn't like getting into trouble all of the time but I just didn't understand or know what to do once I got mad.

"Yup, you are so right Auntie," I said. I grabbed a piece of chicken, my virgin daiquiri, and excused myself to go back into the front room with my cousins who were still playing the game, laughing, and teasing one another over who lost and who looked the funniest while dancing.

After dinner, we all took showers, put our clothes out for school in the morning, and got settled in. We prepared several pallets of comforters and blankets on the living room floor; where we would sleep for the night. We laughed a while longer as we cracked jokes on each other in the dark. The laughter eventually faded out as we fell asleep one by one. I drifted off as I listened to the bubbling sounds coming from the filter of the fish tank as the light eliminated the living room. I can remember it being calming as I laid there in the still of the night.

"Continue," Mrs. Bryant said as she watched me intently.

Well, the next thing that I remember is waking up and my Auntie was coughing. My teenaged aunt who also happened to be there jumped up and fumbled to turn on the lights. My Auntie couldn't seem to catch her breath.

"Here Neicy drink this water. Drink this, it should help." She continued to cough. Panic. Running back and forth from the bedroom to the kitchen.

"Call 911.

Call the ambulance!
(Fear induced chaos)

Dial the number and hurry up!"

At this point all of my cousins were up. No one knew what to do. We sat waiting for the coughing to stop and it didn't. My teenaged aunt was frightened; she began to yell out, "Where are the paramedics! What is taking them so long? Get a wet rag! Get something so that we can put it on her head."

My Aunt continued to cough and gasp for her breath. I could see her from where I sat in the front room however, I was unable to move. I was stuck. I was terrified. I was confused. I was scared. Everything began to move in slow motion as my thoughts swirled around in my head. I slowly found myself in the midst of the chaos walking towards the front door. The screaming and the panic became distant. Their voices faded out. I couldn't see anything. It was black.

I felt a stinging sensation as my vision became more focused. I was crouched down in the hallway of the third floor apartment building with my knees pulled to my chest and my hands over my ears. I heard the screaming again. Everyone was crying and screaming. I was numb. I was crying but there was no sound. I was crying but there were no tears. Where are they? Where is the ambulance? They should have been here by now. It seemed like eternity. Footsteps! I heard footsteps and voices on the walkie-talkies. The paramedics had finally arrived. They ran up the stairs. There I sat still crouching. The door was open. They asked me, "Did you guys call for us?" I couldn't respond. I pointed towards the door. They ran in.

I began to cry as I found myself in that familiar place of grief and loss. Mrs. Bryant handed me the box of tissues that was sitting on her desk.

"How long ago did this happen Bianca, and what hurt you the most about that night?"

I looked at this woman sitting across from me and felt a pain deep in the pit of my stomach. I let out a cry that I hadn't released in a long time. It was gut wrenching. I looked at her and said, "It happened three months ago. Mrs. Bryant I felt helpless. It hurt that I felt so helpless. I couldn't help my Auntie and I knew that things would not be alright. I felt it. I felt it in my heart that I would never be able to see her again. I didn't know what else to do so I ran and I sat in the hallway to be away from everyone."

Mrs. Bryant sat there quietly and reached out to rub my hand. "Bianca, was your Auntie the first person that you ever loss to death? "

"Yes, and she was fine. She was fine so it didn't make sense that she would be taken away from us." Bianca sat for a moment.

Mrs. Bryant asked, "Do you think that you can continue the story or do you feel that you need to stop?"

Bianca had never really shared the loss of her Aunt with anyone and found that although it hurt her to revisit that dreadful night; it also made her feel better to finally get it out. "I can finish," Bianca stated as she wiped the snot from her upper lip.

The paramedics ran in with their equipment and had a black bag that they pulled some things out of. They went into the bedroom and began to push on my Aunties chest and they were calling different codes to one another. One of them came and grabbed some electric shockers and tried to pump her chest like they do on the movies. Nothing. They weren't saying anything. The stretcher. They bought in the stretcher and whisked my Auntie away.

"Where are you taking her?" my teenaged aunt inquired.

"We're taking her to the hospital."

"Take her to St. Francis!" my aunt declared. "St. Francis, take her there." My teenaged aunt made a few phone calls and told us to stay put and that someone would come to get us. She left in the ambulance with my Auntie. I remember watching the lights fade away as they drove into the night and up the long road leading away from the complex.

"Bianca, that was really huge for you to sit through sharing your story about your aunt. Sometimes it takes for us to release it into the atmosphere in order to process the things that are hurting us the most. When we hold them inside they tend to haunt us and sometimes they come out in ways that don't necessarily make sense to us. I honestly believe that some of your anger comes out in such an explosive way because you haven't tried any other form of venting or releasing it." Mrs. Bryant said.

"I am proud of you and I want you to find a way to be proud of yourself. In life sometimes we lose people and it's out of our control. You most certainly cannot go through life living in the past of the; would have, could have, or should have. I'm sure that you miss your Auntie and it sounds like she was an exceptional woman. However, you have to find a way to make her proud of you. Do things in memory of her. Smile when you have a funny thought of her. Cry when you miss her. Just don't stay stuck. All of your feelings are valid Bianca and you have to allow them to come and go."

Bianca felt relieved that she and Mrs. Bryant had connected in a different way. Her unwillingness to let her guard completely down with Mrs. Bryant had shifted and she felt safe at that moment. Mrs. Bryant hugged Bianca and reassured her that pain is only temporary and that she was going to see to it that she was able to deal with some of the things that she had bottled up inside of her. Bianca felt like weights had dropped off of her as Mrs. Bryant stood there and hugged her. She cried for a while longer. Mrs. Bryant held her until she was no longer sobbing.

The Sleepover

Weeks had gone by since Bianca met with Mrs. Bryant and shared about her Auntie's passing. Bianca had begun to display an entirely different attitude. She couldn't really explain it but she felt free. Free to be a teenager. Free to not care. Free to only worry about passing her next assignment in class. Everyone around her had noticed this sudden change. Bianca's mother was proud of her. She was able to go to work and not have to worry about getting disturbing phone calls to come and pick her up or that she had gotten suspended. Bianca was doing so well that she was able to convince her mother and her grandmother to allow her to have a sleepover at her grandmother's house.

It was Friday night after school and we had all made arrangements to stay the night with our grandmother the night before. Gigi's house was known as the go- to- spot or the safe haven for all of us. After making arrangements Bianca along with her cousins knew immediately that they were going to go skating on Saturday night. One by one they had packed their overnight bags and put together the outfits that they had planned to wear to the skating rink where they would be able to interact with their crushes.

Bianca was the last out of the five of them to arrive. "Hey y'all," she said as she walked through the screened in entryway.

Gigi was in the kitchen preparing dinner. "Hey baby!" she said as she checked on her tomato sauce.

"Hey Gigi, I was wondering if my friend Tiara could stay over tonight? You've met her before and her mom lives around the corner."

"Not a problem baby," Gigi responded. "I'm sure she can find a place to sleep."

"Thanks Gigi!" Bianca kissed her grandmother on the cheek and left the kitchen to go tell her cousins that Gigi had agreed to allow Tiara to stay over.

Tiara was everyone's friend. Actually all of the children in Gigi's neighborhood were like family. All of the adults had grown up together and everyone knew everyone's child. Talk about the village. Gigi's development was just that. Therefore, the weekend visits were like one big family reunion. Bianca and two of her cousins left to walk to Tiara's house to tell her that their grandmother was open to let her stay over as long as her mom was alright with it. Bianca and her cousins cut through a neighbor's backyard to get to Tiara's house, she lived one block over from Gigi's house.

Tiara was sitting out on the front step with her brother when the girls finally got to her. "Hey ugly, Bianca called out to Tiara. Our Gigi said that you can stay over. Did you already ask your mom?"

"Yup," Tiara said as she sprung up off of the step that she had occupied. "My bag is already packed." She had the biggest smile on her face as she went in to let her mom know that we were there and that she was about to leave. Tiara came out of the house with her bag and a pillow. "See you tomorrow mom!" she yelled as her mom waved to us through the screen door.

"See you later Mrs. J!" we all said in unison as we made our way back through the neighbor's yard.

Once back at Gigi's, we hung out front of the house talking about what had happened in school during the course of the week and how much fun we had planned to have tomorrow night at the skating rink.

"Tiara, are you going to go skating with us too?" One of the cousins had asked.

"Yeah girl, I already told my mom that I was going with y"all. You know that I have to be a few steps ahead of the game."

We sat around the TV watching *Twilight*, the movie, as we ate Gigi's infamous spaghetti and meatballs. Bianca suggested that they have a dance off. The girls danced and laughed until they all grew tired. Their Uncle came in his fatigues and t-shirt that read Army across the chest; as they were preparing to get settled in. Bianca and Tiara tossed the pillows and cushions from the couch so that they could prepare their resting spot for the evening. It took both of them to pull at the metal rail to get the bed situated. There was nothing like bunking on the couch bed for the night. "Hey Uncle Rex!" we said as he walked past us in the living room with his lady friend close on his heels.

"What's up ladies?" he responded. The two of them headed towards one of the bedrooms down the hallway of the ranch style home. Bianca, Tiara, and one of her cousins looked puzzled as Uncle Rex moved swiftly back and forth up the hallway of the house still with his lady friend trotting behind him.

The girls stayed up a little while longer watching TV on the lumpy mattress. Bianca looked at them and said, "I bet you something is going to happen before the night is over." Bianca had a very strong intuitive side to her. Usually, when she felt that something was going to happen, it generally did.

The girls drifted off to sleep only to be awakened by cursing and yelling coming from Gigi. The red lights on the clock on the other side of the room displayed 3:45 a.m.

"Rex what the hell is going on with you?" Gigi screamed at the top of her lungs. "What on God's good given earth would possess your dumb ass to steal anything from me? Why in the hell would you go and sell my motherfucking TV?!"

"Mom I don't know why I did it. I'm sorry and I'll go and get it back," he said.

"How in the hell are you going to go and get something back? I swear these drugs have totally taken over you. I am so angry with you that I can't stand to look at your ass!"

Bianca stretched as she told Tiara, "I knew it. I told you that something was going to happen." Tiara just rolled her eyes not knowing what else to do or say and covered her head with her pillow.

Gigi told Uncle Rex to leave the house and to take his trifling ass shadow with him. We all knew that she was referring to his lady friend who was standing there looking like a deer caught in headlights. We all rolled over and made every attempt to go back to sleep.

Gigi's house was always crowded. She never told anyone that they couldn't stay. All of the bedrooms were occupied as well as the living room, the couch bed and the floor. There were grown-ups and kids all over the place. Of course, I never being the one to sleep in, was up bright and early as everyone else slept. I got up to go to the bathroom and then came back to my position on the ruffled up sheets and the lumpy mattress that we nested on for the evening.

"Good morning Gigi," I said as she stepped over bodies lying in the living room floor.

"Good morning BJ, you are always up at the crack of dawn! I'm sorry that you had to hear that commotion between Uncle Rex and I last night."

"It's alright Gigi, I had a feeling that something was going to happen, especially since he kept walking back and forth with his lady friend following him."

"Well baby you do know that Uncle Rex is struggling with some things. I just pray that he gets himself together sooner than later." Gigi went into the kitchen to make herself some coffee. It had to be about 7 a.m. As the kettle began to whistle, Gigi and I jumped up to the sound of my Aunt screaming my Uncle's name.

"Rex! Rex! Get up Rex!" she screamed.

Uncle Rex's lady friend and I were on my Gigi's heels. I stood in the hallway and watched as my Gigi and my Aunt screamed at my uncle who had just hung himself. I saw him crouched over on his knees in the closet. He looked like he was praying but I saw the belts strapped together that made his noose.

He was unresponsive as they blew into his mouth and smacked him in the face. I watched as they frantically took the belt from around his neck and propped him up against the side of the bed telling him to get up and that everything would be ok. I watched these events in slow motion as the screams and the movements became distant.

"Call the cops! Rex wake up! He's foaming at the mouth. Close the door! Bianca is standing there. Close the door!"

I was numb and unable to move. I couldn't think. I was crying because my face was wet. "I think he's gone!" I heard them say through the closed door. Then I heard my Gigi scream….. "Rex, oh Lord, what have you done?!"

I slowly walked back into the living room where all of the other kids were up sitting along the edge of the sofa bed with looks of horror on their faces. "I think Uncle Rex killed himself," I said as I sat down in an empty spot on the sofa bed.

The sirens where loud as the paramedics and the cops simultaneously pulled up in front of the house. They went into the room where Uncle Rex, our Aunt, and Gigi were. It seemed like they were back there forever. Tiara was scared and asked if we would walk her home. She gathered her pillow, her bag, and the blanket that she had bought with her. We walked her home in her pajamas and told her that we would call her later if we were still going to go skating.

We silently walked back to Gigi's house uncertain as to what we all were thinking or feeling.

Once we got back to the house we put the sofa bed away and placed the pillows and cushions back in their rightful place. Gigi's house was chaotic. We sat there wondering how much longer they would be in the back and if and when Uncle Rex would be taken to the hospital. They came from the back room with Uncle Rex on a stretcher covered from head to toe with a white sheet. How traumatic!

The phone kept ringing and our parents were starting to arrive. As they loaded him into the ambulance people were starting to gather in the front yard, cars were parked everywhere, and people were talking, crying, and screaming. Once the ambulance drove away; the cops put yellow tape around the front of the house and instructed everyone (family) to go back inside. They began to question my cousins and I about the events that took place leading up to this morning. They asked who all was there. They stated that we had to go get Tiara and that she was to go with us to the police station; where the questioning would continue.

Bianca sat in the back of the car on the way to the police station. Peace never lasts long, she thought to herself. In her head Bianca thought of all of the reasons that Uncle Rex could be so selfish. He had never been a selfish kind of man. However, he decided to take his own life in a house filled with kids and not to mention his own mother. What would make a person do such a thing? Bianca felt the anger creeping up on her and the tears filling up in her eyes. Bianca was now back in that dark place that she was still working towards escaping from.

SCHOOL

That Monday in school, Mrs. Bryant noticed Bianca sitting at the lunch table alone. "Hello Miss James, how was your weekend and why are you over here alone and away from your girlfriends?"

"I had a long weekend," Bianca responded in a tone that Mrs. Bryant was familiar with.

"Well do you want to talk about? We can have lunch in my office."

Bianca wanted to go to the office with Mrs. Bryant just so that she didn't have to sit in the cafeteria and explain to everyone why she was acting different on this particular day. She grabbed her bag and her lunch tray and followed Mrs. Bryant to her office.

Bianca started crying as soon as she sat down. She had walked around all morning trying desperately to not allow a single tear to fall. Mrs. Bryant was surprised at how emotional Bianca was and waited patiently for her to share what was bothering her. Bianca stood up with tears streaming down her face and shaking her hands as if they were wet from washing them. "Mrs. Bryant, why does my life have to be so crazy? I'm tired of everything. My uncle hung himself over the weekend and I was there! I saw him hanging there! It's too much! I can't get the vision out of my head. They expect me to act normal. I don't understand." Bianca stood there crying and shaking with snot and tears running down her face.

Mrs. Bryant grabbed some tissues and wiped Bianca's face. She was at a loss for words given that they had just recently touched on the passing of Bianca's aunt. Mrs. Bryant knew that at this very moment Bianca just needed to get it out. She didn't want to hear anything she just wanted someone to listen, and that's exactly what Mrs. Bryant did.

Friend in Crisis

Phone rings...

"Hey girl what are you doing?" the voice asked on the opposite end of the phone.

"Nothing, just watching BET. Why? What are you doing? Bianca asked Shantelle.

Shantelle had a way of making things more dramatic than what they really were. She always went from one extreme to the other. It was hard for her to maintain solid friendships. Given that Bianca was one of the very few people who would confront Shantelle. The friendship that they had established worked.

Shantelle began to go into a list of things that had been bothering her. Bianca listened to her rant as she continued to watch 106 and Park on BET. Bianca enjoyed watching the dance routines and listening to the beats behind the music. She really didn't care one way or another what the song was really about.

"Are you listening?!" Shantelle screamed into the phone.

"Girl hush, I heard everything that you said!" Bianca yelled back at her. Shantelle picked up right from where she left off.

Before long Bianca heard a shift in Shantelle's voice. It was an unfamiliar tone. She sounded distant and hopeless. "Girl, what is really going on? Why do you sound so sad? Why does what you're saying not make any sense? I told you how to deal with the pressure of the changes at home and your boyfriend. I know that you're all messed up in the head about your dad leaving. Girl, dads leave all the time. It doesn't make it right but it happens. Heck, I even know a few moms who have left. It might hurt now but you learn how to deal with it. And, that crazy, stupid, piece of crap boyfriend of yours; he's so not worth the headache." "Boys our age cheat all the time. My mom always says that they don't really know what they want so they fool around with multiple chicks until they eventually figure out what they really like. My life isn't easy either but I want something out of it and I also see us growing old together. So get your life and stop being so dramatic. You sound like it's the end of the world!"

Shantelle began crying and talking really fast. By now they had been on the phone for two hours and Bianca was really tired.

"Shantelle, girl, please tell me what is wrong with you! It is 11 o'clock and you're not being up front with me about some things."

Shantelle continued to sob as all of her words were running together. Bianca was getting angry. She did her very best to not add fuel to the fire and pleaded with her friend to tell her what the real issue was.

"I will be better off dead! Shantelle blurted out.

Bianca heard her loud and clear this time. "Shut the hell up! What makes you think that dying is the answer? This situation that you are dealing with is only temporary. It won't be like this forever! Shantelle, you know how I feel about people talking about wanting to die when there is so much to live for. You know what we just went through with Uncle Rex. You were there! I think it's selfish and inconsiderate of people to talk about wanting to die! I still have nightmares sometimes.

I can't believe that you would say such a thing. Damn you Shantelle!"

Shantelle continued to cry as she shared with Bianca that she had just taken a bottle of pills. Bianca became enraged as she began to scream at Shantelle. "Why on earth would you do that? Who is at home with you? What kind of pills did you take and how many? Do you feel sick? Should we call the ambulance? Should we call the cops? Shantelle, I can't believe that you would do that! What were you thinking? Go put your finger down your throat!"

Bianca's thoughts were all running together as she thought about the day that she saw her Uncle Rex hanging from the closet. Bianca knew that she couldn't get off of the phone with Shantelle. Therefore, she continued to talk to her just to make sure that she didn't drift off to sleep into some pill induced coma that she could possibly never wake up from.

Bianca pushed to stay awake and in tune with Shantelle. There were several periods of silence. However, the two of them managed to stay on the phone until 6 a.m. Bianca's alarm clock began to ring as it was her usual time to get up. Shantelle, I will see you in school in a little bit so that we can talk about what just happened. Shantelle agreed and they got off of the phone with one another to prepare themselves for the school day.

Bianca stood in front of the mirror in the bathroom, eyes bloodshot red, and tired from pulling an all-nighter to ensure that her friend was safe. Bianca began to cry as she stood there feeling angry, hurt, and helpless herself. I am so mad at her for pulling me into that. Why would she do that? She knows how I feel about that shit and she chose to pull me into her mess. Bianca cried as she showered trying to figure out a plan. She knew that she would be uncomfortable being around Shantelle today and felt that she wasn't really quite ready to face her.

SCHOOL

Once in school Bianca made every attempt to avoid Shantelle. Bianca took the long way to class; walking outside of the school building to get from one class to the next. Bianca took the back stairwells to ensure that she didn't have to face her. Bianca knew that Mrs. Bryant would know what to do. She was the only one in the building that she felt safe enough with to tell what Shantelle had done last night. Bianca managed to find Mrs. Bryant who had been in meetings for a majority of the morning.

"Good morning Mrs. Bryant," Bianca said as she greeted her.

"What's wrong Bianca?" Mrs. Bryant inquired because of Bianca's demeanor. "Why do you seem so agitated?"

"Can I please talk with you? Not out here in the hallway, can we go to your office?" Bianca said as she kept looking around still trying to keep Shantelle at bay.

The two of them walked into Mrs. Bryant's office where Bianca began to pace back and forth. "Go ahead Bianca tell me what is bothering you," Mrs. Bryant said in her calming tone of voice.

Bianca began to cry. "I don't even know where to start! Oh my God, I am so mad at her!" Bianca yelled as she continued to walk back and forth across the floor of Mrs. Bryant's office. Mrs. Bryant sat there patiently waiting for Bianca to share what was weighing so heavy on her.

"Mrs. Bryant, can you believe that Shantelle took a bottle of pills last night! I haven't had any sleep! I was home, minding my business and she called. Everything was going fine and then out of nowhere she told me that she had taken the pills. I don't know what kind or how many. I just don't understand why she would do such a thing!" Bianca continued as she reflected on the conversation from the night before.

It was clear to Mrs. Bryant that Bianca was traumatized over what Shantelle had done. "Is Shantelle in school today Bianca?"

"Yes, she is," Bianca stated. "I've been avoiding her all morning because I feel like I just want to punch her in her face for doing that!"

"Well, Bianca," Mrs. Bryant continued, "punching her in her face is not the answer. However, you coming and telling me what happened is. We will get Shantelle the help that she needs and you can best believe that you did the absolute best thing for her by telling."

"Then why do I feel so horrible? Why am I so angry with her?"

"Probably because Shantelle's attempt at ending her life took you back to you witnessing your Uncle's suicide.
It's perfectly normal for you to feel the way that you do and your feelings are valid. I would be upset too if a friend of mines

made an attempt to harm herself while I was on the phone with her. In fact I would be outraged!" she stated still in her calming voice.

Bianca began to feel a little better as the conversation continued and Mrs. Bryant reassured her that Shantelle would be alright. Mrs. Bryant checked in with Bianca emotionally to make sure that she was alright to return to class.

Mrs. Bryant got on the phone and called Shantelle from class to come to her office immediately. The bell rang and Bianca thought that she was doing good in her avoidance antics, but this time when she got to the top of the stairwell; there was Shantelle. Bianca's heart sank to her feet. "Hey girl," she said although it may have come off extremely awkward.

She felt awkward and uncomfortable standing in front of Shantelle. Shantelle, informed Bianca that Mrs. Bryant had made a call and that she was going to have to go away for a few days to see where she stood mentally. Shantelle hugged Bianca and said, "Thank you so much for telling. I know that you are mad at me but I am glad that you told. At first I was upset with you for telling but after speaking with Mrs. Bryant, I completely get why you did what you did and I appreciate you for that."

Bianca wanted to hug her back, but she couldn't bring herself to lift her arms to do so. She was still angry and she was extremely uncomfortable. Bianca asked when she would be going to get the help that she needed.

Shantelle informed Bianca that the "people" were on their way. However, she asked Mrs. Bryant if she could be excused to find Bianca and to thank her.

Bianca was at a loss for words. The two girls stood there looking at one another for a few seconds before Bianca broke the silence. "Good luck with everything. I hope that they can figure out what's going on with you and that you get everything that you need. I guess you can call me when you get home."

Shantelle hugged Bianca again and headed back towards Mrs. Bryant's office as Bianca headed towards her next class. Bianca's mind was flooded with thoughts. She was good at masking so she was able to get to her advanced reading class and jump right in.

Kenny saw Bianca as he walked past her class. She noticed him and immediately smiled. For some strange reason she felt like they connected on some other stuff.

EBONY MADDREY MS

Bianca wasn't really into boys, however felt comfortable enough to interact with Kenny. He told her to meet him after class in front of the band room. Bianca waved her hand as if to tell him to go on about his business. He smiled at her and said, "I'll see you in a little bit."

Bianca had a difficult time staying focused on the series they were reading about Shakespeare and a sonnet from Romeo and Juliet. Her mind constantly drifted to the thought of what Kenny wanted with her after class. Bianca couldn't bring herself back to reality, although she tried on several occasions. She began to daydream about being with Kenny intimately, her own love story, and how it would end.

The room was dimly lit and everything was covered in white. There were white sheets, shag rugs, curtains, candles of different heights and widths. Bianca stood there as everything flickered from the glow of the candles. Bianca was even dressed in a white gown that was airy and flowed down past her ankles.

She floated over to the bed and laid there observing the beauty of the room. Kenny walked in with only white lounge pants that hung from his waste. Their eyes connected and Bianca took a deep breathe not knowing what to expect as he walked closer to her. He knelt over her and kissed her on her cheek and then on her forehead. Bianca let out her breathe as she raised her hand to palm the back of Kenny's thick black wavy hair.

The bell rang.........

Bianca glanced around the classroom as she snapped out of her lovely daydream. She wondered if anyone one else in the room could tell what she was daydreaming about and if they were aware of her mental experience of losing her virginity. Bianca gathered her things and clumsily trotted towards the door to leave.

The teacher, Mrs. Calhoun, stopped Bianca at the door. "Bianca James," she said to her. "I'm not exactly sure where you were today, but it was clearly obvious to me that you had checked out mentally during class. Whatever you are dealing with Miss James, I want you to know that you can talk to me. I will do my very best to assist you. You cannot afford to lose sight of where you are headed in life Bianca, and I have noticed for quite some time now that you have been preoccupied with your thoughts."

"Thank you, Mrs. Calhoun. I do have a lot of things going on and I will do my best to get back on track. I will let you know if I ever need to talk."

Bianca excused herself as she thought, she's crazy if she thinks that I would share anything about myself with her; get the hell out of here. Bianca turned the corners of her lips up at the thought of confiding in Mrs. Calhoun as she headed to the band room to meet up with Kenny. Kenny was standing there grinning at Bianca as she walked towards him. This made her a little uncomfortable.

"Why are you always smiling like that when you see me?" Bianca asked Kenny.

"Because „B", you are so damn fine! Sike! Nah, I just think that you are one of the smartest girls that I know and I like that about you."

"Well thanks. I would like to say that you are one of the smartest guys that I know but unfortunately I can't!" They both laughed out loud as they stood in front of the band room.

"Why did you want me to meet you here Kenny?" Bianca inquired as she tried to shake the thought of her recent daydream that involved him.

Kenny looked at her and smiled again. "Well B, I really just wanted to see you before my next class. It's just something about seeing you that makes me feel funny on the inside." Bianca stood there blushing. She knew exactly what he was talking about because she had the same internal feelings.

"Boy you had me walk all the way down here just so that you could see me?! Bianca said in her most sarcastic tone.

"Yes „B", I did." Kenny said unsure of how to take her response.

"Well Kenny, why not just take a picture!" Bianca turned to the side and struck a pose. "Go ahead, pull out your phone and take a picture!" They both smiled. Kenny reached in his backpack, grabbed his phone, and took a few shots of Bianca as she gave him a few poses.

"There you have it. A mini photo shoot of yours truly," Bianca said as she looked him in the face.

"B, I also wanted to know if you wanted to go out with me?"

His comment totally caught her off guard but she impulsively said, "Yes!"

The two of them stood there for a moment before Bianca excused herself by saying, "You know what? I have to get to class. The late bell is about to ring. I'll talk to you later." Bianca turned to walk away.

"Aye, yo „B"!" She turned back to look at Kenny who was standing there grinning again. "It's you and me baby!" He said as he blew her a kiss by holding two fingers up to his lips.

Oh my god, Bianca thought as she walked to her next class. Did I just agree to go out with Kenny?! What a day! Shantelle is on her way to the crisis center and Kenny just asked me out.

THE BLENDER

The First Time

Bianca and Kenny had begun to hangout a lot; going to the movies, staying up on the phone, visiting each other at home. It was a beautiful spring day and Kenny had met Bianca at the ice cream shop where they went frequently to purchase sundaes and talk about everything. The talked about who was doing what to the most recent song that had been released.

"Hey, Mr. Tao, can I get a small caramel sundae with nuts and whipped cream? Keep the cherry though," Bianca said as she looked through the ice cream display of all of the newest flavors.

Kenny scoped out the display as well before placing his order. "Yeah, Mr. Tao, and I'll have two scoops of the peanut butter cyclone on a waffle cone with chocolate syrup, whipped cream, and I think I want my cherry. Actually, Mr. Tao, you can give me her cherry too!"

Mr. Tao smiled at the two of them and their obvious like for public displays of attention. Bianca and Kenny both laughed at the comment Kenny made about taking both cherries.

They found a spot in the corner of the small quaint shop after Kenny paid Mr. Tao for their ice cream. Bianca sat so that she could look out of the window to take in the scenery. Kenny of course positioned himself so that he could stare at Bianca and admire the way that the sun beamed off of her beautiful skin and made her eyes look lighter than what they really were. "It's so pretty outside today," Bianca said as she began to eat her sundae. Kenny didn't really respond he just gazed at her as she ate her ice cream and he ate his.

Bianca was caught up thinking about her reoccurring daydream of being with Kenny in the white room and how her first experience could possibly go. "Yo B! What are you over there thinking about?" Kenny inquired as he stood up to readjust his pants.

Bianca was startled and felt a tad bit embarrassed at the same time. "Boy sit down! You're always in someone's thoughts!" They smiled at each other.

"B, I was thinking that we could hang out at my place when we leave here. My mom is at work and I just picked up a few movies."

"Sure that sounds like a plan." Bianca replied.

They left the ice cream shop and headed out towards Kenny's house. Bianca was having all sorts of conversations in her head at this time and likewise, so was Kenny. For whatever reason, this time heading to Kenny's house made both of them feel somewhat nervous. Bianca desperately tried to mask the anxiety that she was feeling as she counted her breaths in her head. It was a technique she had learned during her visit to the Children's home.

Kenny was thinking about all of the ways that he could entertain Bianca without making it obvious that he too was nervous about her coming to hang out while his mom was not there. It will be different this time because we have access to the whole house. I sure hope that I don't make a fool of myself, he thought as they continued on their walk.

The air was fresh and the sun shined on all of the leaves in the trees. Kids were outside playing jump rope, ball, and riding bikes. There were several landscapers out cutting grass and putting down fresh mulch. The smells and sounds were nice, although they weren't enough to distract either one of them from the world wind of thoughts taking place in their minds.

The split level home, occupied by Kenny, his mother, and his younger brother, who was away for a weekend camping trip; looked like something straight out of the *Home and Garden Magazine*. The tan house had large stones on the exterior and metal lamp posts. There were several Japanese maple trees scattered about the front yard. Their purple leaves were pretty. There were small clusters of plants and flowers evenly lined across the front of the house. The grass was nicely manicured and trimmed evenly. Bianca followed Kenny up the driveway as he led her around to the side of the house so that they could enter from the side door that led to the family room.

Kenny immediately stepped out of his sneakers and took his t-shirt off. He was now only wearing his beater/white tank, jeans, and sweat socks. Kenny looked at Bianca and told her to make herself comfortable. "Do you want something to drink B?" Kenny asked. "We have grape juice, soda, and water."

"I'll take a bottle of water," Bianca said as she unstrapped the brown gladiator sandals that she was wearing. The gray carpet felt soft under Bianca's feet.

Bianca found herself drifting off again into her pure white experience. She felt herself getting warm on the inside. Just as she began to envision what it would be like to finally kiss Kenny, he reentered the room with her water and a few snacks.

"Ok „B", I have two comedies; a love story, and a horror flick. Which one would you prefer?" In the back of his mind Kenny knew that Bianca was going to choose the love story. She absolutely surprised him by saying that she preferred to watch one of the comedies.

Kenny pulled out *Along Came Polly*, claiming that it was his all-time favorite. Bianca looked at him and said,

"Boy that is not a new release!"

"I know B, but it's hilarious and I could watch it over and over again."

Kenny got up and put the DVD in the player and sat back down next to Bianca on the gray sectional. Kenny had his feet up on the couch and pulled Bianca close to him so that they were in a reclined position. She sat with her back next to his chest and sunk back into him as her support. She took in the scent of his Hollister cologne. Likewise he inhaled the fresh scent of her freshly done hair.

Neither one of them was able to focus on the movie as the sounds blared through the surround sound system in the family room. Kenny tried desperately to distract his thoughts of Bianca's soft skin and inviting her into his room to really lay next to her. He tried to focus on the humor in the movie to avoid from having Bianca feel his building erection.

"You know what „B"? I think that I want to take a nap. I'm getting a little tired. Do you want to stay or do you want me to walk you home?"

Of course Bianca didn't want to leave. She wanted to spend more time with Kenny. It didn't matter if he was entertaining her or not. "What time is your mom expected to come home Kenny? I would never be able to face her if she caught me napping in her house."

"Well dang „B", it's not like we're going to be freaking or anything! Now that would be embarrassing! Although, I would like to freak you, but I know you're scared," Kenny said to Bianca in a sarcastic way. He flashed that big smile at her as she punched him in the arm.

"Boy quit! I am not scared of anything and I darn sure ain't scared of your little worm!"

Kenny frowned at her and said, "Little? Girl please I have a snake! An anaconda at that!"

They both laughed. Bianca couldn't even imagine what Kenny's magic stick looked like let alone what it would feel like. All she knew was that her white vision did not include any snakes of any size. Kenny jumped up and told Bianca to follow him to his room. "My mom is working late tonight so she won't be home until after 9. You have nothing to worry about. We're good and I promise not to take advantage of you."

As they headed up the stairs towards Kenny's room Bianca began to wonder whether or not she was setting herself up for some sort of disastrous turnout or if it would be possible for both of them to keep their hands to themselves and not do something that they both would end up regretting.

One step at a time, Bianca began to feel the butterflies lose control in her stomach. One step at a time, she began to see her mother's face and hear her mother's voice about saving her virginity and how boys only want one thing. One step at a time, she began to see Mrs. Bryant and Kenny's mother who both viewed her in such high esteem. One step at a time, she heard the voices of her friends encouraging her to get her cherry popped. One step at a time, Bianca was uncertain about what would come next. One step at a time, she felt that she couldn't change her mind and let Kenny know that she should probably head home.

Before she knew it she was standing in front of Kenny's bedroom door. He showed her where the bathroom was just in case she needed to go. Bianca needed a moment and turned and walked into the bathroom. Once inside she sat on the toilet and stared at herself in the vanity mirror.

Oh my god! I am about to go into Kenny's room. What in the world am I thinking? I don't want him to think that I am a punk. So I can't back out. Bianca convinced herself that she had everything under control. She stood up to fix her cloth- ing and washed her hands as she continued to look at herself in the mirror. I can handle this. Nothing is going to happen and if he tries, I'll just tell him that I am on my period.

Bianca felt confident enough to finally exit the bathroom. Kenny had turned his iPod on and had Drake playing through the Bluetooth speakers. He had lit a few vanilla scented candles. Bianca was amazed at how clean his room was (to be a boy). She smiled at him and said exactly what she was thinking. "Wow, you actually have a really clean room to be a boy!"

"My mom wouldn't have it any other way "B". She's something like a neat freak. I swear she has a little OCD. Kenny's room was mature and organized. He had one wall covered in posters of rappers, athletes, and girls in swimsuits. There was a nice sized flat screen TV mounted to the wall over top of his dresser. His décor was gray, green, and white. Kenny had nice window drapery that was coordinated with his comforter and throw rug in his room. It was nice and very relaxing. It wasn't the white room that Bianca found herself visiting frequently in her mind.

Kenny stepped out of his pants and put on a pair of gym shorts. Bianca was again shocked that Kenny was not ashamed or embarrassed to be in front of her in his underwear. Kenny sat on the edge of the bed and admired Bianca as he watched her survey his room. "Come on „B", come over here. There is nothing special in this room except for you."

Bianca was through surveying the room. She was actually trying to calm her nerves and to revisit her breathing exercise without being obvious. She went over and sat on the edge of the bed next to Kenny. He grabbed her hand gently and began to kiss her on her cheek. Bianca was captivated by the sounds of the music coming through the speakers, but was unable to make out who was singing and what they were singing about. Kenny's kisses went from her cheek, to her neck, to her shoulder. Bianca was caught up and was enjoying the attention that Kenny was giving her. Kenny wasn't sure of how this would all play out nor did he know what he was doing. He knew that it felt right and that he was enjoying the response that he was getting from Bianca.

Kenny saw this moment playing out just as it had played out in the movie that he watched with his older cousin Tyaire. Tyaire had always been the one to put Kenny on to how to approach girls and how to get them to give in to him. As Kenny continued to kiss Bianca, he was able to reflect on all of the lessons that Tyaire had given him. Kenny was proud that he was able to keep his nervousness under control. All he knew was that he didn't want to stop and that he intended to go all the way.

Kenny began to rub on Bianca's chest and she didn't stop him. Her thoughts were racing but she didn't want this moment to end. Once Kenny noticed that Bianca's breathing had changed he pulled away from her and asked if she wanted him to stop. At this point she couldn't think straight, she couldn't see straight, and she didn't want to stop feeling what she was feeling. Kenny whispered in her ear that he would stop if she was afraid. "Here we go again," she said in a panty voice. "I am not afraid Kenneth."

Kenny stood up in front her with a full-fledged erection. Bianca looked at the anaconda and thought to herself Oh my! What am I going to do with that? Kenny walked over to his closet and pulled out a shoebox that was filled with little black and gold packages. One thing Tyaire did was provide Kenny with his own stash of condoms so that he would never have an excuse of not being prepared. Kenny had practiced for months how to put a condom on with one hand; while looking, while under the covers, and while in the dark. Tyaire always taught him that it's better to be prepared so that he won't look like a clown in front of a girl when the time came for him to lose his virginity. Kenny was ready.

He walked back over to Bianca and put the condom on the bed. He looked at her and said, "Are you really ready for this?

Bianca wasn't sure but the words escaped her mouth before her brain could process anything. "Yes, I am ready. I've been ready," she added unsure of how this would really go down.

Kenny pulled the covers back and motioned for Bianca to climb in. Bianca awkwardly laid back into the

sheets and pulled her panties off. He was surprised and climbed into the bed with her after dropping his shorts.
Bianca turned her head at the thought of touching Kenny's private parts. He realized that Bianca was more nervous than he was and resorted to kissing her again. Bianca was unable to relax and tensed up as Kenny's penis rubbed against her thigh. He refused to check in with her again to inquire about her being certain about doing this. He did not want to risk Bianca changing her mind. Kenny managed to slide out of his underwear and to put the condom on.

He began to fool around to figure out exactly where to put it. With a little force and effort, he found his way into Bianca's temple. Kenny was in heaven and Bianca was trying to mask the pain that she felt when the anaconda finally made its way into her cave. Kenny began to move around awkwardly while the beauty of the white room had diminished in Bianca's mind. She drifted off to the dark room at her grandmothers, and it before she knew it, it was over.

Kenny rolled off of her and kissed her on the top of her head. They both laid there, not knowing what to say. Bianca had the comforter pulled up to her neck because she didn't want Kenny to see her nakedness. Her thoughts flooded her head as she thought to about what just happened.

The tears began to well up in Bianca's eyes as she desperately tried to fight them off. Kenny saw the stream of tears running down the side of her face and didn't know what to do. Tyaire hadn't prepared him for this. He began to wonder if he had hurt her or if he did something wrong. Was it whack, he wondered? Boy, this was the best moment of my life and now „B" is over there crying. Kenny took a huge breath and put his arm around Bianca. "Talk to me „B"," he pleaded with her. "Tell me what's going on and why you are crying?" Bianca couldn't answer him because she really didn't know what she was really crying for. She wiped her face, got up to gather her things, and told Kenny that she was going to walk home, alone.

Girl Fight Gone Wrong

After hanging out at the pool all morning with Veronica and Tiara, the girls agreed that they would go and get something to eat.

"Hey BJ, what's really going on with Shantelle? We heard that she was acting a little loopy."

"Well, she was just overwhelmed and dealing with a lot of different things. It kind of spiraled out of control and she felt like she wanted to give up," Bianca responded.

"Damn, is she in the crazy house with the crazy folk?" Veronica asked as she mimicked a mummy.

"V, you really should stop clowning around all the time. It's really not funny and she needed some help. I don't think that they are crazy I just think that they need a little assistance in making better choices. That's all. I mean heck, I get tired and overwhelmed all the time. But after what my family went through I would never want to put that kind of burden on any of them. Shit my grandmother still isn't back at 100 after my Uncle."

Tiara looked over at Bianca as she had a sudden flashback of the night that Uncle Rex took his own life. She nudged Veronica and told her, "Enough already V, all that matters is that Shantelle is getting help. Where did we decide to eat?" Tiara questioned in an attempt to change the subject. Veronica took the hint and said that they all would meet up around two o'clock, so that they could catch the bus over to California Tortilla.

At two o'clock promptly, the girls were all standing at the bus stop waiting on the DART bus to head up Rt. 1 to one of their favorite spots. They clowned around and talked about who and what was happening. The girls noticed a swarm of people running towards the park. "What in the hell is going on? Veronica said. They all looked at each other, shrugged their shoulders, and headed towards the commotion.

The crowd was so heavy that it looked like a riot. People were screaming and climbing over one another. Cop cars were everywhere. There were little kids, teenagers, and adults all gathered around. What's going on? What has happened? Who is fighting?

"Break it up! Break it up!" the police yelled. After a while all of the chattering sounded like bees buzzing. All of the voices were becoming distant. You couldn't make out anything that anyone was saying.

Screaming.

Yelling.

Crying.

Looks of panic.

Why??????

All you could hear at this point were muffled voices. Bianca and her friends were able to piece together that there was definitely some sort of girl fight going on. Veronica was hyped and screaming right along with the crowd.

"Dang!!!! What are all of these people down here for? It must be some heavy hitting going on!" she said as she jumped up and down smacking her fist into the palm of her other hand.

"Chill V, it has to be major since all of these cops are coming. I can't see it being a girl fight with this much coverage. It has to be a couple of guys."

"Maybe someone got shot?" Tiara said.

"I'm not sure but this shit is bazooka!" Bianca said.

The cops began yelling through a bullhorn for people to move away from the area. They were still trying to get to the heart of the fight. It was indeed a group of girls fighting, three on one. It appeared that the one who was huddled in the center was crouching over. As the crowd continued to move away it became clear as to what was going on in the center of all of the chaos. The three girls backed away and took off running. There was blood everywhere. The girl in the middle just fell over. As the screams continued Bianca was able to

make her way through the crowd on the sidewalk now and realized that it was one of her cousins.

Bianca began to scream frantically but the cops would not let her near the young girl who was lying in the street soaked in blood. Bianca made every attempt to fight against the strength of the police officer that was in between her and getting to her cousin. "Sharae!!!!" Bianca yelled at the top of her voice. "Sharae, get up baby! Sharae I'm here."

Sharae lay   there   unresponsive. Bianca was screaming, kicking and crying. "Let me go! Damn it, let me go! Sharae! Sharae!"

The paramedics came and began to do CPR on Sharae. She still was not moving. Everyone was standing around in total shock as these two people tried effortless to do their job in bringing this young lady back. After what seemed like hours they lifted Sharae's body up onto the stretcher put her in the ambulance, turned on the red, white, and blue sirens, and drove away in a hurry. The cop was still blocking Bianca who was distraught from being restrained. When she turned around her mother was running up behind her. Bianca just fell limp into her mother's arms as she sobbed. "Mom, I think that they killed Sharae! She wouldn't move Mom! She wouldn't move!"

Tiara had called Ms. James after she realized that Sharae was involved in the fight and that Bianca was losing control. They all piled into Ms. James" navy blue

Sequoia and drove to the hospital. Ms. James made a few calls to various family members telling them that something had happened to Rae and that they needed to meet her at the hospital. She was short with each person simply telling them that she didn't have all of the details but they needed to stop whatever they were doing and get there. Bianca sat in the front seat that swallowed her small frame up sobbing silently with her head pressed against the window. Veronica and Tiara were quiet and occasionally glanced at each other as a way of checking in.

Once they arrived at the hospital there was a lot of commotion going on in the waiting area. Other family members had arrived before they had gotten there and everyone was frustrated because they didn't know what was going on. The nurse behind the station kept repeating herself each time someone walked up to the window to inquire about the condition of Sharae. "I'm sorry. I cannot release any information at this time. Once her parents arrive then they can tell you what the patient's condition is." Of course it came off very cold and insensitive. However, the nurse was simply doing her job.

Ms. James called her brother several times to see how far away he was from the hospital. He was coming from West Philadelphia, taking him a little longer than everyone else to arrive. Ms. James looked at the three girls and saw that they were scared and confused about what they had just witnessed. She took them all by the hand and said calmly, "Bow your heads so that we can pray for Sharae." They all did it without hesitation.

> *"Father God, we come to you in the need of prayer. We are asking for peace and understanding as to what went wrong on this day. God, I ask that you cover Sharae and guide the hands of the doctors who are in the back working on her. God, I ask that you touch the lives of the young people. God, I ask that you allow them to see that fighting is not the way to go. Father God, I come to you humbly in that all things work together for your good. I know that this is a touchy situation God, but you know the plans that you have for us. Father God, comfort the*

*hearts and minds of Bianca, Veronica, and Tiara God. Allow them to know that you will put a hedge of protection around them Lord, simply because I have asked you too. God, make it known to them in the simplest terms that you Lord, are Jehovah Nissi and there is no need for retaliation God. El Shaddai, cover and protect them in the Lord Jesus Christ name I pray. Am*en"

The girls" faces were drenched in tears as they all said amen in unison. Ms. James began to pace back and forth. Bianca knew that although she and her mother didn't always see eye to eye that if someone was in need of prayer that she would have one ready. People were sitting everywhere in the waiting area. There were friends of Sharae's who were crying and talking about the fight and how Sharae was beating all of the girls up. Then one friend was talking to one of the guys standing there and said that someone had an army

knife and that by everyone crowding around the fight you really couldn't see what was going on. When Bianca heard the word army knife she began crying hysterically all over again. "Mom I think that the blood was from Sharae being stabbed!" She screamed and put her head in her hands.

Veronica and Tiara sat there crying, but they both were at a loss for words and couldn't find anything to say in that moment. Bianca's uncle stormed through the double doors of the emergency room and went straight to the window. "Hi, my name is Jax James and my daughter is here," he said to the cold nurse as he struggled to catch his breath.

Bianca's mother walked over to him as they waited to be cleared to go into the back. The nurse looked at her and asked, "Are you the mother?"

"No, I am her aunt," Ms. James replied.

The nurse looked at her and said, "Then I cannot allow you to go into the back."

Uncle Jax looked at her and said sternly, "This is my sister damn it! My daughter's aunt, and she will be permitted to visit with her niece damn it! Now show us where to go!"

The nurse said a few things to them and buzzed them in to go in the back. The automatic doors closed slowly behind them. It seemed as if they were in the back for a very long time. Bianca and the other girls had drifted off to sleep while waiting to hear something. When uncle Jax came through the door slowly Bianca could tell that he had been crying. Her mother emerged from behind uncle Jax and her eyes were red and swollen as well.

Bianca jumped from her seat and walked towards her uncle and her mother. She stood there silently waiting for them to share what had went on behind the double doors. "BJ," her mother started, "Sharae did not make it. Apparently, she was stabbed multiple times and one of the cuts was along one of her major arteries. Sharae lost way to much blood and was not able to hold on any longer." Uncle Jax stood there speechless as he reached to hug Bianca who stood there tensed and silently crying. They hugged one another and cried until they both had no more tears to shed.

Ms. James signaled to Veronica and Tiara so that she could get them home. The car ride was quiet and all of the girls were speechless again, as this was the youngest person that any of them had known to die from a simple girl fight.

SCHOOL

The following week in school Bianca was extremely quiet. She did not feel like being bothered and she was also preoccupied in thought with the upcoming funeral for her cousin. While sitting in class, the lessons were all a blur. Bianca had difficulty focusing on what it was that the teachers were saying. She was quiet during lunch and would sit at the lunch table picking at her food. She had no desire to eat anything.

Tiara and Veronica tried to cheer her up but were very unsuccessful. Kenny tried to be supportive but Bianca pushed him away. It was too much. She hadn't really talked to him much since he ruined her idea what it would be like doing it for the first time. Bianca was uncomfortable with the thought of having "did it" and it not being what she had expected. This was extremely trying for Kenny but he felt that he couldn't press the issue given that she had experienced several losses in such a short period of time.

While changing classes, Marketta, one of the school bullies was messing with Tiara. She kept saying smart comments about Tiara's weight and how Tiara thought she was cute but that she'd mess that cuteness up. Now everyone in the school knew that Tiara was not a fighter. Tiara tried to ignore the girl. Having a hard time getting a reaction from Tiara, Marketta snatched Tiara's gold necklace off of her neck and threatened to take every piece of jewelry that she owned. Tiara stood there looking and feeling helpless as the tears began to form in her eyes. Bianca knowing the relevance of the gold necklace that belonged to Tiara's great grandmother, snapped.

Bianca stood up and cornered Marketta. "I can't stand your punk ass!" Bianca yelled as she began punching and kicking Marketta. Bianca was screaming at Marketta, "I'm sick and tired of you always fucking with people that you know are afraid of you! Bitch, I'm going to show you today! You have messed with the wrong one!" Bianca was oblivious to the crowd that had now formed surrounding her and Marketta as the fight continued. Marketta didn't

stand a chance. Bianca released all of her pent up anger and frustration right there in the hallway. Marketta was crouched over from embarrassment and fear. She had never been the one on the losing end of a fight.

Security came to break up the fight. When they got there Bianca was still swinging, yelling, and cursing. Marketta stood up and spit a glob of blood out on the floor. She had nothing to say and walked away before the guard could grab her.

The crowd stood there quietly as many of the bystanders were in disbelief that Bianca had just handled one of the biggest bullies in the school. Tiara ran over and picked her necklace up off of the floor. She felt bad for Bianca because she had never seen her go to such an extreme.

As the security guard took Bianca away she locked eyes with Kenny. He just stared at her. Bianca turned away. She could not wrap her mind around what Kenny may have thought about her at that very moment. Bianca was unsure as to what caused her to get so angry. She tried to justify her outburst by saying that Marketta deserved to get beat up because she was always bullying weak people. Bianca didn't intend for the fight to become so brutal. She simply wanted to let Marketta know that enough was enough.

While waiting in the Principal's office. Mrs. Bryant received word that Bianca had just been involved in a fight. Bianca heard the clickety-clack of high heels on the tile floors. She knew instantly that it was Mrs. Bryant.

Mrs. Bryant entered the office wearing a beautiful red suit with a multicolored scarf draped around her neck and some multicolored Jimmy Choo pumps. Mrs. Bryant stood in front of Bianca for several minutes without saying a word. Bianca stared at her silently, not knowing where to start or what to say. Deep in her heart, Bianca knew that she had disappointed Mrs. Bryant, again.

"Bianca Renee James! What in the world were you thinking of to beat that girl up like that?! I cannot believe that after all that we've discussed that you would succumb to that kind of animalistic behavior. I keep telling you that you are a young lady and not an alley cat. Bianca, young ladies do not fight with their hands. We fight with our brains. I am

beyond disappointed and you have a lot of talking to do. I cannot continue to back you up and to advocate for you when you run around this building without displaying any sense of self-control!" Mrs. Bryant stood there now with irritability written all over her face. "BJ, I need you to get it and I need you to get it now! I need you to understand that you and only you determine your own future!"

Bianca sat there absorbing each and every word that escaped from Mrs. Bryant's mouth with tears streaming down her face. Mrs. Bryant had to look past the tears. Although, it hurt her to see Bianca in so much pain, she needed Bianca to understand that this kind of behavior will have her dealing with a lifetime of regrets and foreseeable failures. "Start talking young lady," Mrs. Bryant said as she positioned herself to listen to whatever justification Bianca could drum up.

Bianca cleared her throat and looked down at the floor. She was unable to look Mrs. Bryant in the face. She began with, "I know I should have…"

Mrs. Bryant cut her off before she could finish. "Excuse me Bianca, but I'm standing in front of you. I am not down there on the floor. If you want me or anyone else to take you seriously then you need to work on making eye contact no matter how uncomfortable it gets. You look people in the eye when talking. Do I make myself clear?" "Yes," Bianca replied. She sat up in the chair that she was originally slumped over in, cleared her throat, looked Mrs. Bryant in the face, and began again. "I know I should have walked away and informed the proper people about Marketta and her picking on everybody. I was just angry that she took Tiara's great grandmother's necklace and I knew that Tiara was too afraid to stand up to her. I was already bothered thinking about my cousin's funeral and whether or not I was ready to face that."

Mrs. Bryant stopped Bianca. "What cousin and what funeral?" Bianca shared with Mrs. Bryant through her sobs about the recent death of her cousin. At this point Mrs. Bryant was able to sympathize with Bianca and began to talk about all of the fear, anger, and unresolved emotions behind loosing someone so young and so close.

After talking for quite some time, the Principal was ready to discuss the consequences with Bianca. Mrs. Bryant

accompanied Bianca into the Principal's office to help soften the blow and to possibly advocate for an alternative punishment.

Dr. Berhman began by saying, "Bianca James so I hear that you've had another outburst, this time seriously hurting

another student. You know from previous incidents that the school policy does not condone fighting or putting others at risk."

"Yes, Dr. Berhman, I do," Bianca replied. Dr. Berhman had already talked with several of the other students to gather details leading up the fight and everyone's account was pretty much the same.

"Well, Miss James, I'd like to hear from you and how it is that you are now sitting across from me. So begin from the beginning," he said.

Bianca sat up straight, looked Mr. Berhman dead in the eyes, and began to give her account of what had taken place. Mr. Berhman was pleased to hear that Bianca's account of what had happened lined up with the other stories that he had heard prior to speaking with Bianca.

Mrs. Bryant asked if she could add to Bianca's account as well. "Most certainly Mrs. Bryant, I trust your insight and feel that it may even help in making my final decision pertaining to how I'm going to deal with Miss James," Dr. Berhman stated. Mrs. Bryant shared the pressure placed upon Bianca in dealing with three deaths this school year and her commitment to doing community service at the Children's Home to assist in dealing with some underlying emotional issues. Mrs. Bryant also shared that Bianca is related to the young lady who was recently killed in a girl fight. The story was featured on all of the news stations, therefore, Dr. Berhman knew exactly what she was referring to. Mrs. Bryant also shared that the funeral was scheduled to take place at the end of the week. Mrs. Bryant even went a step further to say that she would take personal responsibility for any future altercations that Bianca may find herself in.

Bianca could not believe that Mrs. Bryant would put herself on the line for her. Personal responsibility means that if I do anything then Mrs. Bryant could go down, Bianca thought to herself. Bianca was angry with Mrs.

Bryant for doing this because she wasn't sure if she could keep her end of the bargain. Bianca didn't want anything or anyone to get in the way of the relationship that she had formed with Mrs. Bryant. At that very moment Bianca made an internal vow that she would make better choices and that she would work even harder to control herself no matter what.

"Well, well, well," Dr. Berhman stated. "Miss James you are a lucky young lady. Mrs. Bryant has definitely gone beyond her call of duty to show her level of confidence in you. Given that she has put herself out there for you and given that she believes you're worth it. I am going to trust her judgment. I am going to give you three days of in-school suspension, you must continue with community service, Mrs. Bryant will contact Ms. Washington to add six more weekends of service. You will be put on a behavior contract, and you will check in with Mrs. Bryant during your study hall two times a week. You better not let her down and you better not find yourself in my office under these circumstances again. Do I make myself clear Miss James?"

"Yes, you do Dr. Berhman."

"Good because the next time that you're in my office it will be your last because you will be expelled. Mrs. Bryant, take her to your office please and contact her mother. She has to be picked up today and the in-school suspension will begin tomorrow. You ladies may be excused," Dr. Berhman said.

Although, Dr. Berhman cut Bianca a break Mrs. Bryant was still upset with her. Bianca thanked Mrs. Bryant for putting herself out there. "I promise Mrs. Bryant I won't let you down. I promise that I'm going to do things differently."

"You better young lady, because at this point, you decide. You decide if it's going to get better or worse. I pray that this is the last time that I have to tell you this."

While waiting for her mother, Mrs. Bryant reached in the bottom drawer of her desk and handed Bianca a beautiful purple journal. "I think that it's time that you begin to write about what's hurting you, what's hindering you, and what has you so guarded. Write every day or at minimum two times a week. Bring your journal when you

come to meet with me. You can read directly from it or you can summarize what you have written. Bring it with you so that I can verify that you're actually writing. I see so much potential in you BJ and it hurts my heart to see that you have no idea of how great you can be."

FUNERAL

The day of the funeral was rainy and somber. Bianca woke up from a horrible dream to the sound of the rain tapping on her window. The view from her window was gray. She could see the trees swaying back and forth. Bianca laid in bed pulling the white and coral comforter up over her head. I'm not sure if I can do this she said to herself. I don't want to see Sharae like this. Will she look like herself?

Auntie didn't look anything like herself and neither did

Uncle Rex.

Tears began to swell up in Bianca's eyes as all of these thoughts swirled around blending together in her head. Bianca continued to lay there feeling like a blender, crushing all of the single thoughts into one big concoction of fear, confusion, and anger. Bianca's mother entered her room slowly. She sat at the foot of her bed and rubbed

Bianca's leg. "Good morning BJ, do you think that you are up for this today?" her mother asked.

Bianca didn't want her mother to know that she was crying under the covers, so she continued to lay there silently trying to pretend to be asleep. Ms. James knew that Bianca was awake, given that she has never slept past seven o'clock since she was a little girl. "BJ, I know that you have a lot of emotions running through you right now, with all that has taken place in the last three months. I think that everyone will understand if it's too much for you to attend the services today."

Bianca couldn't contain herself any longer and let out a loud screeching wail. Her mother knew the exact pain that she was feeling and sat there rubbing her leg until Bianca

was through. "As I said BJ, you, the family, us, we've all been through so much in such a short period of time. What you must understand is that in due time the pain will become easier to deal with. What you are feeling at this moment is completely normal and understandable. Losing people is always hurtful. Take a little while and decide if you want to

go or if you want to stay behind." Ms. James stood up, kissed Bianca on the forehead, and walked towards the door. Ms. James turned around as she got closer to the door and said to Bianca, "BJ no matter what we go through I never want you to doubt how much I love you." Bianca was caught off guard by her mother telling her that she loved her. She hadn't heard that in a very long time.   Bianca tried to remember the last time that her mother hugged her, let alone tell her that she cared about her. "I'm about to hop in the shower to get myself together and I'll be back to check on you."

Bianca rolled over on her side and continued to sob as she watched the raindrops trickle down the glass on the window. I have to go to the funeral she told herself. There is no way that I'd ever be able to forgive myself if I didn't go. After several minutes Bianca kicked the covers back, now laying on her back staring at the ceiling. She took several deep breaths, sat up, and said "Sharae, this one is for you

Boo! See you soon."

She turned on her iPod, hooked it up to the speaker on her dresser and began to listen to Jayz and Beyoncé *On The Run*. How appropriate, Bianca thought as she thought about her and Sharae laughing, singing, and rapping songs by the two of them. After showering, Bianca brushed her hair up into a bun, put on her stud earrings, and put on a little eyeliner. Dressed in her black dress she walked downstairs to leave the house with her mother.

As they pulled up to the church, there were cars parked everywhere. There were people filing in and out of the church. Several news reporters were stationed outside. Bianca put on her black Versace shades as she walked towards the double doors of the sanctuary with the rest of her family. Bianca was uncertain of what she was feeling at

the moment that she stepped foot inside of the church. The people around her were a blur. The conversations taking place were muffled. The usher walked the family in. As they got closer to the casket, Bianca felt like she was suffocating. Her knees felt weak, her head was hot, and she felt like she was about to vomit.

Sharae's mother was screaming and yelling, "Get up baby! Get up from there! She's just sleeping, wake up! Wake up Rae!" Bianca felt like her legs were in cement. With each step towards the casket, she felt as though it was a struggle. Once at the foot of the casket, Bianca caught a glimpse of Sharae. She looked like she was ten years older than she really was. She was dressed in a dress with flowers all over it, something that Sharae would have never worn.

Her hair was curly like a rod set, Sharae would have never let anyone set her hair. Bianca felt faint.

Sharae's skin tone was darker, her lips were puffy with pink lipstick on them, Sharae never would have worn lipstick, and her face was swollen as well. "Oh my god where is my cousin?" Bianca thought. Her mouth was dry like cotton and she could not believe her eyes. Bianca stood on the side of the casket sobbing uncontrollably. She remembers losing her balance and someone catching her. Bianca blacked out and couldn't remember the rest of the funeral service.

FLASHBACK

After watching the premier of the Nutty Professor on HBO with all of her cousins, Bianca decided that she was ready to go to bed. While everyone was in the family room making Rice Krispy treats and brownies, she made her way down the hallway. Stepping out of her sweatpants, putting on an oversized t-shirt, and climbing into the full-sized bed; Bianca pulled the covers up over her shoulders. She

scooted close to the wall so that she wouldn't have to move by the time her cousin came.

Bianca was in a deep sleep and had no idea that her cousin was lying next to her. She was awakened by fingers fumbling around in her panties the movement woke Bianca up out of her sleep. She was afraid and immediately tensed up. "What are you doing?" Bianca questioned her female cousin. However, no sound came out of her mouth. Bianca desperately tried to pretend that she was still sleeping. Afraid and confused at the same time; Bianca clamped her legs together tightly.

The breathing of her cousin got heavier. "Open your legs a little," she whispered to Bianca. Bianca was so tensed and didn't want her cousin to know that she was not asleep. Is this really happening? Why Me? Bianca had so many questions flood her mind. Bianca continued to pretend to be sleep and pretended that this was not really happening. In her mind she fled. She was not present mentally. She just wanted it to be over.

REVELATION

The Bottom Line

Now back at the Children's Home, Bianca was angry all over again. She was angry that more time had been added to her initial contract. What in the world was Dr. Berhman thinking to suggest six more weeks of community service she thought to herself. Dang, that's a heck of a lot of time to spend with these people. He is so extra all of the time. Bianca pressed her head against the back of the seat trying to mask her anger and frustration. It was really too early to hear her mother go into all of the "it's your fault", "you know better", and "you should have thought about the consequences". Bianca knew what to expect this time and had already purposed that she would willingly participate so that the time would go by a lot faster than it had on the weeks where she hadn't participated before.

Ms. Washington was waiting for her at the front door when Bianca arrived. Bianca looked over at her mother as she leaned over to reach for the handle on the car door. "See you at four, mom," she said and noticed that her mother was holding the steering wheel super tight and looked straight ahead.

"See you later BJ. I sure hope that they help you with some self-control." Bianca rolled her eyes, got out of the car, and headed up the walkway towards Ms. Washington. Bianca knew that she had disappointed her mother yet again.

"Good morning Bianca, I received a call from Mrs. Bryant and she shared that you would be spending a little extra time with us here at the Children's Home. I am so glad that you are able to grace us with your presence. I feel that you have a lot to offer and also a lot to learn." Ms. Washington said.

Bianca smirked as they walked through the front doors of the building. I just love this building, it's so peaceful, she thought to herself as she admired the blue and white décor and the sense of being at the beach. Although Bianca was there to carry out her sentence of community service, she felt safe each time she entered the building. "Ms. Washington, is there anything that you need me to do before we get started today?" Bianca asked.   "No dear, I just want you to give all of yourself when we start our sharing circle today."

Bianca just stared at her. "I guess, if you say so." Ms. Washington looked back at Bianca and smiled. "Miss James the only way for you to move pass your past is to confront it head on. You have to be like an eagle flying towards the storm. He tucks his head and goes for it, but when he comes out his head is held high and his wings are expanded. That's his way of showing the world that he has survived the storm and that he has come out victorious. In life Miss James, we have to choose whether we will come out of our storms as victors or victims.

"Now I am pushing the envelope in saying that I believe that your anger and all of your outbursts are the result of something that you have witnessed or from something that

139

has happened to you directly. I don't need you to answer me I just want you to think about it. When we give a voice to the dark places in our lives they can no longer haunt us. So whatever, it is that has been holding you back dear you need to give it a voice, give it some light, and find your voice along the way. You have so much to offer not only yourself but you have a lot to offer this world.

Bianca didn't know how to respond. She did, however, know that what Ms. Washington said about the eagle put things into perspective for her. Wow, Bianca thought I am just like the eagle, but I've been using my strength to show other people that I am not a punk and that I am not weak. Bianca knew at that moment that she was done fighting all of the time. She was through being angry and wanted to release all of those things that had been hindering her. She knew that it was time to share with her mother about those things that took place late at night when everyone was sleeping. But how?

Simone, who was the first person that Bianca connected with at The Children's Home, walked through the doors. "Good morning Ms. Washington, good morning Bianca."

"Good morning Simone," they both said at the same time.

"Simone why don't you and Bianca go ahead and head back to the garden and get the chairs arranged. The others should be trickling in shortly." Ms. Washington instructed.

The girls headed out to the foyer that led out to the garden. They talked about the various things that had transpired since they last saw each other. Bianca was relieved to hear that things had not been as problematic for Simone as they had been for her. "Simone, I am so glad that things are starting to work in your favor. What changed for you and at what point did you realize that you were no longer angry."

"Well I'm glad you asked because I was planning to talk about that today during the sharing circle. So talking to you now will give me practice." They both laughed but knew that Simone was serious and that Bianca truly wanted to know.

Simone began by saying, "Since coming here to the Children's Home and working with Ms. Washington, I have begun to look at things and life completely different. I don't let too much get under my skin. Ms. Washington is one of the most amazing people that I have ever met. She helped me to understand my worth and to also understand that my anger was starting to work against me. Then she gave me this speech on how important it is to give hurtful feelings a voice in order to move past them. I never looked at it like that until Ms. Washington taught me about that concept. I always thought that people would judge me if they knew certain things about me. I felt that I wouldn't be accepted for being myself. I also felt that I would make myself vulnerable in sharing certain things."

"When I learned that all of the things that had happened to me, and all of the things that I have experienced, where not any fault of my own, I felt better. I felt free. Most of all, I felt happy for the first time in a long time." Simone stated.

Bianca stopped moving the chairs and stood there looking at Simone. "Girl, I honestly don't know what happy feels like or even what it looks like. I feel like I've become numb to that feeling. Even when I am smiling or with people that I care about, I still don't feel happy," Bianca said.

Simone understood where she was coming from. "I will tell you this Bianca, if you hang around here long enough and if you listen to the things that Ms. Washington says to you, trust me you'll feel happy again." Bianca smiled at the thought. She walked over to get the basket of ribbon to put in the center of the chairs that she and Simone had arranged in a circle in the middle of the garden.

The chairs began to fill quickly and before long all twelve chairs had a body sitting in them. There were some new faces along with some of the more familiar faces. Today felt different. Bianca asked Ms. Washington, after she had given her greeting and the new members were welcomed, if she could start today. Each person in the circle grabbed their ribbons and went back to his or her seat. The instructions again were given to name someone or something that has hurt you in the past and to state whether or not you had forgiven yourself or the person for whatever pain the situation caused.

As purposed, Bianca planned to fully throw herself into today's discussion. Bianca stood up, took a deep breath, and exhaled. "Hello, my name is Bianca, my family and friends call me BJ, of course this wasn't a part of the script but Bianca was nervous. When I was younger I was molested by not only my grandmother's boyfriend but by one of my closest female cousins as well. Most of the time we only look as males as being perpetrators but there are a lot of female perpetrators as well. I never realized how much of those situations affected me today and are most likely the reason why I am the way that I am."

Ms. Washington was proud of Bianca for standing up and sharing and knew that this was probably the most that she had shared about what had happened to her. Although, normally it is a quick check in for each person she felt the need to allow Bianca to continue.

"I fight all of the time. My mom feels that I am a constant disappointment. "I am always angry," Bianca began to cry. "I never knew why I did the things that I did until now. It all makes sense to me. Both Simone and Ms. Washington said something to me today and it caused a lot of things to bubble up inside. I've never shared this with my mother because I didn't know how. I wasn't sure if she would believe me. I wasn't sure if I deserved what had happened to me, and I wasn't sure if I was strong enough to share. But now that I have finally given the dark place a voice, I found out that it isn't as scary as I initially thought it would be. I am not completely sure if I have forgiven either of them or not. I'm sorry that I took up so much time but I want to thank you all for listening."

As Bianca turned to tie her ribbon to the young lady sitting next to her she realized that everyone in the circle was crying too. Ms. Washington stood up and hugged Bianca. "Thank you so much for sharing Bianca I am glad that you trusted us enough to let us in." The other participants in the circle continued the process and Bianca sat there feeling liberated amongst her peers. After the events of the day: the sharing circle, mural painting, cleaning up, lunch, and socializing the clock read three forty-five. Oh my goodness Bianca thought, what happened to the time. Ms. Washington came over to where Bianca was sitting and wanted to do one final check in with her before leaving for the day.

"So Bianca, she started, is it ok for me to call you BJ?" Bianca was surprised. She really hadn't thought that anyone picked up on her trying to stall in the beginning of sharing circle when she announced what her family and close friends called her. Does this mean that Ms. Washington is now a close friend?

"Yes, it is fine for you to call me that," Bianca responded and let out a huge radiant smile that she couldn't contain.

"Well BJ, I must say that I was thoroughly impressed with you today. I feel as though you gave 110% of yourself today and I also feel that maybe there was a little relief that you experienced. Am I correct? I could be wrong."

"No Ms. Washington, you are absolutely on point. I was hesitant at first but I kept hearing you and Simone in my ear about giving feelings a voice. Also, when you said the thing about the eagle this morning. I was like, wow, I am an eagle." Bianca laughed as the words escaped from her mouth. "Ms. Washington without you and Mrs. Bryant, I don't know if I could have ever seen myself being in this place or even being brave enough to share what happened to me. The only thing left for me to do is to finally share with my mom. I think it will help her to understand me a little bit better."

"Well BJ, you read my mind. I was thinking the same exact thing. If you are ready we can have you share with your mom when she comes to get you in a little while." Bianca became anxious, but knew that she had to push through it. "As long as you understand that none of it was your fault and that your mother can't protect you from the things that she is unaware of. As parents, we do everything in our power to protect our children and sometimes the people we should be worried about protecting them from, are the people closest to us."

Bianca agreed and felt that it was time. She knew that it would be a lot on her mother given that they just went through all of the deaths and changes in the family. Bianca also felt that by having Ms. Washington there, things would go a lot smoother.

Exposed

Bianca's mother pulled up and parked in front of the building. Ms. Washington was standing at the front door.

"Good afternoon, Ms. James," Ms. Washington said. "Do you have a moment to come in and talk? I have some new discoveries that I would like to include you on."

Ms. James smiled at her and nodded as she released her seatbelt to get out of the car. What in the hell did this girl do today? I am so over this nonsense she said to herself as she walked towards Ms. Washington. The women walked into the building together. When they entered Ms.

Washington's office Bianca was already sitting on one of the cream colored couches.

"Hey mom," she said as her mother entered the room. "Hello BJ," Ms. James said trying to cover up what she was really thinking.

"Please take a seat Ms. James," Ms. Washington said as she extended her hand towards one of the comfy chairs.

Ms. Washington sat in a chair directly across from Ms. James. "Ms. James, I asked you to come in because Bianca did a fantastic job today." Bianca's mother was relieved. "She was able to share during one of our activities and some things surfaced pertaining to her younger years."

Ms. James was back on edge. "I hope this isn't about her father Ms. Washington, BJ and I have been down this road several times and I will not allow his absence to continue to be the reason that she is acting out."

"I understand where you are coming from Ms. James, but this however, has absolutely nothing to do with her father or his absence." Bianca sat quietly as she began to wonder if this was a good idea to let her mother know about Delvin and Nika. "Well, excuse me Ms. Washington, but I am really confused," Ms. James declared. "Did BJ get into another fight and you are trying to soften the blow? Did she freak out on someone that you need her to apologize to? If not, can we just cut to the chase and get to the bottom of this impromptu discussion?"

"Absolutely Ms. James, we will get right to the point," Ms. Washington respectfully stated. "Bianca dear," Ms. Washington restarted. "Would you please share with your mother the same things that you shared today?" At this point Ms. James was sitting on the edge of her seat not knowing what to expect from her daughter.

Bianca began to feel all hot and sweaty. She felt the sweat beads ball up in the palms of her hands. Internally, she was a nervous wreck and couldn't tell if her mother and Ms. Washington noticed that her breathing had escalated. At this point Bianca was rubbing her hands back and forth across her knees in an effort to calm herself down and to wipe away the wetness that had developed. Bianca shook her leg vigorously as she took a deep breath to tell her mother what she had already shared with Ms. Washington earlier. "Well mom, I've been holding a lot of stuff in for a really long time. Can you promise not to say anything until I am completely finished?"

Ms. Washington chimed in, "Ms. James with all due respect, I think that is pretty fair of Bianca to ask."

Ms. James was thinking to herself, if this woman does not shut the hell up I am going to smack the shit out of her. "Ok, go ahead BJ talk. I'm listening."

"I wanted to let you know that I was touched when I was little."

Ms. James clenched the straps on her pocketbook trying to stick to the agreement of not saying anything. "Go ahead BJ, continue."

"It happened a few times and I tried to always block it out of my mind. I didn't want to think about it and I didn't want to get into trouble. I didn't feel like you would believe me." Bianca began to cry when she saw the tears coming down her mother's face.

"Who BJ? Who touched you?!" Ms. James sputtered as she stared her daughter in the eyes.

Ms. Washington allowed the two of them to go through the process. Bianca looked away from her mother and looked up at the pictures and articles up on the wall in the office.

That was her way of avoiding the tears and the piercing gaze of her mother. "Who BJ?! Tell me who touched you!" her mother yelled.

"It was Delvin mom. Delvin and Nika."

"What in the world?" her mother said. "How? When? Where BJ? How when did this happen. I am going to kill those mother fuckers! Why didn't you tell me? I am so sorry BJ, all this time you've been walking around with this. Oh my God!!!!" Ms. James continued to sob as her thoughts ran through her head. Ms. James jumped up off of the chair and ran over to Bianca and hugged her. She held her tightly and the two of them stood there together in the center of Ms. Washington's office crying. "I am so sorry BJ, for not knowing."

"I am sorry too, for not saying anything mom. I was scared, and I didn't know what you would think of me. I didn't know what to think of myself." Bianca sobbed.

Ms. Washington sat silently until Bianca and her mother released their grip from one another. "Ms. James, I apologize that you had to find out this way. However, I am also amazed at the courage that it took for Bianca to share that with you. It is my hope that we can continue to work through the process. I can assist you two in getting through such a difficult and traumatizing thing. I feel that the more the two of you are able to talk about this and to figure out which way that you want to go with regards to pressing charges, will allow Bianca to be free of the things that she has been holding in for so long."

"Mom please don't press charges! I don't think that I am ready to deal with that. I want to do things the right way and focus on being able to find a place within myself where I can forgive the people who hurt me.

"That is really big of you and mature Bianca," Ms. Washington stated. "However, it may come to the point that charges may have to be made. I will continue to work with you during community service. I would also like to begin family therapy with you and your mother. Ms. James, do you think that this is something that you would be willing to do?"

Ms. James was still in shock from what she had just heard. "Delvin though? And Nika? Damn! How did I not know?" her mother questioned.

"Ms. James, sometimes, things get away from us and most perpetrators are extremely crafty. They know how to manipulate and control their victims in such a way that it's confusing and hard for the victim to figure out. Is there any possibility that Delvin will have access to BJ?" "No, Ms. Washington," Ms. James said. "Delvin is dead, he's been deceased for a few years now."

"What about Nika? Do either of you feel that she is an immediate threat at this time?"

Both Bianca and Ms. James both responded, "No," at the same time.

"How old were you BJ?" Ms. James asked. The pain in her eyes showed the pain that she must have been feeling in her heart.

"It started when I was about three of four with both of them. It lasted a little longer with Nika."

"How old were you when it stopped BJ?" Her mother inquired trying to remain calm.

"I don't know mom, I guess I was eleven."

Ms. James sat on the couch, crying.

Ms. Washington began to speak again, this time, making it a point to try and comfort Ms. James in not feeling guilty about what has happened. She shared with her that she simply trusted the people that she had left her daughter in the company of. She explained that there was no way of knowing that any form of molestation would have taken place. Ms. Washington was able to get Ms. James to a pretty good place emotionally. "Again, I would like to meet with the two of you for family sessions at least for the next three weeks."

Ms. James agreed, gathered her purse and her daughter and stood to make an exit. "Before I go, I just want to apologize, Ms. Washington, for how I came off towards you. It's just that BJ and I have been through so much and I am so used to getting disturbing phone calls about her behavior. Thanks to you, it all makes sense now. I feel so bad that my daughter has been walking around screaming for help and I totally ignored all of the signs, because I was dealing with my own stuff. Words cannot express the amount of gratitude that I have for you right now. Thank you for helping BJ and for agreeing to help me to help her." "No, thank you Ms. James," Ms. Washington said. "My job is to help others help themselves. So thank you for trusting me and allowing us to go through this together. Bianca has a really bright future ahead of her. Therefore, you've done a lot of things right momma. Now I know that this has been very draining for the both of you. Go home, have a wonderful dinner and get some rest. You have my number here so feel free to call me should the need arise; if not I will see both of you next week."

The car ride home was awkward. Bianca wasn't sure what to say to her mother and her mother wasn't quite sure what to say to her. Ms. James reached over to grab Bianca"s hand and whispered, "I'm so sorry baby for not protecting you."

Bianca looked over at her mom and cried out, "It wasn't your fault, and you had no way of knowing!"

"I just wish that you had told me sooner." Ms. James thought to herself about all of the outburst from Bianca and all of the trouble that she had been in over the years. She thought about the nasty attitude and the „I don't care" way of dealing with life. Ms. James rubbed Bianca"s hand with her thumb with one hand and continued to control the steering wheel with the other. "BJ, I am so sorry. From now on, there will be no secrets. I want you to share everything with me even if you feel that I will be mad. There is nothing that you can say to me that will make me stop loving you. I know I don't say it often but I love you and you mean everything to me. I would completely lose my mind if anything ever happened to you." Bianca looked over at her mother and saw that her face was drenched in tears. Bianca cried silently, sunk back into her seat, and held on to her mother's hand as they drove through the city to get home.

I Finally Got It

That night Bianca wrote in her beautiful purple journal for the first time. She couldn't wait to share with Mrs. Bryant about what took place and how right she was about sending her to The Children's Home to do community service. Bianca now viewed Mrs. Bryant as her guardian angel.

God knew what he was doing when he gave me you... she started as she began her first journal entry. Before she knew it, Bianca had filled up six pages in her journal. She wrote about telling her mother about the molestations, having sex for the wrong reasons and it not being a good experience, feeling that her mother hated her for all these years, dad leaving and starting another family, and not feeling worthy of being happy. Bianca wrote about how none of that stuff mattered any longer. How she finally gets it, and how important it is for her to look at life through a completely new set of eyes.

Triumph

Breakthrough

Junior year went by really fast. Bianca and her crew were preparing for senior pictures and senior prom. Bianca and Kenny had a few ups and downs in trying to make things work. Kenny had a hard time understanding Bianca, her mood swings and her discomfort in having sex with him. He figured that he'd fool around and she'd never find out. However, as the year progressed Kenny stopped going to school, started smoking weed, and Bianca didn't have time for the challenge of trying to keep him around.

She no longer argued with other people over him and found herself constantly arguing with him. Halfway through the year it was rumored that he had two babies on the way.

After approaching Kenny about the rumors, and him being so disrespectful about it, Bianca decided that she was through with him. That situation almost bought up a lot of emotions that Bianca had tucked away; rejection, betrayal, distrust, anger, emptiness, etc., but she refused to allow it. Bianca was still meeting with Mrs. Bryant on a weekly basis and had now moved into a peer mentor role within the school. It gave her a sense of gratitude to be able to model the things that she had learned from working with and watching Mrs. Bryant. She felt like she was able to mediate and help her peers the way that Mrs. Bryant and Ms. Washington had helped her.

Mrs. Bryant began to push Bianca into thinking about college and the importance of wanting to be successful. Mrs. Bryant also recommended that Bianca consider becoming a Debutante. Of course, it was foreign to her. However, whatever Mrs. Bryant suggested Bianca knew that deep down inside, it would benefit her in some form or fashion. Bianca wanted to know if Mrs. Bryant could recommend that her friends participate as well, so that she wouldn't have to do the program alone.

"Bianca James, sometimes in life, we have to endure our journey without the people who are closest to us. It's important that you understand that you cannot always take people with you. You will be blessed to meet new people and to formulate new friendships along the way. Never be so closed minded that you don't allow yourself to explore what other people have to offer."

EBONY MADDREY MS

Moving Forward

Senior year, Bianca threw herself in completely. She did what she needed to do to become a Debutante, applied to several colleges (a little later than most of her peers), sat for the SAT"s, and stayed away from as much drama as possible. Bianca joined a couple of clubs in school, obtained a job, began to repair her relationship with her mother, and began to establish a relationship with her father who had been in and out for most of her childhood.

In spite of how the first three years of high school played out and all of the issues that Bianca had bought with her, she was selected to speak at the graduation. It was an honor. To a certain degree she felt that many of her peers were more deserving. Bianca had learned over the years about how much power one possesses when given the opportunity to speak and how powerful a message can be. She was determined to make her trials and tribulations heard in an effort to motivate or encourage her peers the way that she had been motivated. She wanted to relay a message that would let others know, acting out is not the best way to deal with your problems. Bianca spent weeks preparing the rough draft of her speech. She wanted to receive insight and feedback from both Mrs. Bryant and Ms. Washington. She knew that she wanted to make her mother proud given that she had caused her so much grief and heartache.

It all became real once Bianca received her cap and gown. I can't believe that this day is finally here, she thought to herself. Bianca was in her room admiring herself in the full length mirror. Her mother walked by and saw her with the cap on, she stood in the doorway and began to cry. When Bianca noticed that her

mother was watching her she turned and looked at her. "Oh my God, Mom! Why are you crying? It's really not that major, it's just a graduation cap," Bianca stated.

"Baby it's more than a cap. BJ you have made it! It's been a hard road and I swear I never really counted you out. You are my child and I knew that you would eventually get it. I am beyond proud of you and words cannot express what this graduation means to me," her mother said.

"Mom you are being extra with it!" Bianca said as she smiled at her mother.

Prom came and went, senior cut day was a total blast, and now it was time to walk across the stage. Bianca had mixed emotions. A part of her felt happy and excited to finally be done with high school. The other part of her felt sad and uncertain about moving forward. What would that mean for all of her friendships? What would that mean for her daily encounters with Mrs. Bryant? Who would be there to pull her back in if she happened to go back to her old ways? Again, all of these thoughts began to swirl around and blend together in her head. Bianca knew that at this very moment that she could not allow the anxiety that she was feeling to overtake her. She began to do some of the breathing techniques that Ms. Washington had taught her to regain focus. Bianca sat on the side of her bed and practiced her speech silently in her head. Then she practiced out loud in front of the mirror.

The Next Phase

As the students began to arrive into the stadium Bianca felt a sense of pride and accomplishment. She knew her speech inside and out and felt that many of her classmates would be able to relate. If they weren't then, they would definitely know someone who could. The band began to play and the speakers began to march towards the stage. Bianca thought that her heart was going to jump out of her

chest because it was beating so hard.

She was able to calm down a little once she spotted her family in the audience. She felt even more at ease when she saw Ms. Washington sitting in the audience with a huge poster board and a bullhorn. After the band stopped, the stadium grew quiet. Dr. Berhman acknowledged the students for all of their accomplishments and wished them well on their future endeavors in life. He shared with the crowd who would be speaking and why they were selected.

"First we will here from Bianca Renee" James. who has made tremendous strides over the past four years. We all have watched her evolve into a beautiful young lady. It was a little bumpy in the beginning, but I must say that we are all so very proud of her and what she will go on to do in

life."

Bianca sat back not realizing that she would be the first to speak. She went into her mental place of tranquility and reassured herself that she would do just fine. Bianca stood and made her way to the podium. She braced the edges of the stand as she looked out over the stadium filled with her classmates and their families. After the applause died down, Bianca took a deep breath, and began to speak:

"Good afternoon, I just want to start by congratulating all of you and your successful completion of this journey. I understand fully now that my story may not necessarily be your story, and that your story may not necessarily be mines. I do know however, that we all have one thing in common and that is officially being a part of the 2014 graduating class of Colonial High. When I first got to Colonial, I was an angry little girl. I had very little ambition, and I had very little hope that I would be in the position to walk across the stage. I found myself in many fights along the way. I had so many feelings pent up that I didn't know what to do with them. So I did what most teenagers do, I acted out. I defied the rules, I disrespected adults, and more than anything I disrespected myself. I can remember walking the hallways and feeling like I didn't belong, feeling like everyone else was better than me, feeling like no one would ever believe in me. Until the day that I met a special woman who turned my outlook on school and life around. She helped me to understand that in life we can't always blame the people around us for our shortcomings. We have to learn how to be more accountable for our own behaviors and actions. She taught me that there is a consequence for everything in life based upon the choices that we make, whether they are good or bad. After meeting her, I began to look at the idea of attending school a little differently. I began to feel like I was a part of a caring community. I was officially a part of the Colonial family and from that moment I figured that I needed to get my act together. I learned that sometimes it isn't the message, it's the messenger. Often times as teenagers, we ignore the advice or insight that is given to us by those who care most because we feel like they don't understand and that we can figure it out by ourselves.

Now that we have all reached the crossroads where we have completed high school and we are trying to figure out which road we will take, whether it be going off to college, attending trade school, going into the military, or enter directly into the workforce; it is

167

important that we think long and hard about these decisions. We must realize, in the words of Mrs. Bryant, "That we determine our own future." So although, your beginning may not have been as chaotic as mines, and even if it has, at this very moment, the only thing that matters is that I made it! You made it! We made it!

I wish you all much luck and success in the future and I look forward in seeing everyone at our ten year class reunion. Thank you all for staying committed to yourselves in completing one of the most memorable tasks in life. Congratulations again to us! The graduating class of 2014!"

Everyone stood to applaud Bianca for her wonderful delivery. She noticed that Mrs. Bryant was sitting in the front row smiling with tears in her eyes. She nodded in approval as Bianca took her seat. Bianca also noticed that her mother was wiping her face when she glanced over at her. She was relieved and proud of herself for being able to pull her speech off. After the rest of the speakers spoke, it was time for the graduates to receive their diplomas. The band began to play again, as they all lined up and walked across the stage one by one.

The families were all gathered inside of the reception tent where they greeted the graduates. Bianca navigated through the crowd until she found her mother.

"Hey mom, what did you think of my speech?" Bianca asked.

"I thought it was absolutely beautiful baby, you did an exceptional job!" Her mother said. "I have some more great news for you too BJ." "What is it?" she asked.

"Well the mail came today while you were here preparing for graduation. You received a letter from the University of Delaware."

Bianca was confused because she knew that she had applied really late to all of the schools of her choice. "Well what's good about it mom? Did I get accepted?"

"Even better," her mother said as she handed Bianca the envelope addressed to both of them. Bianca opened the letter and stood there amongst all of the chaos as she read the letter silently. "Oh my God, mom! Are you serious? They gave me a full scholarship! Mom I can't believe it!" Bianca screamed at the top of her lungs.

Bianca hugged her mother and yelled, "I'm so excited! This is the best news ever!" "I have to tell Mrs. Bryant!" Bianca said. "I'll be right back mom," Bianca said as she scanned the faces under the tent. When she saw Mrs. Bryant, she took off running through the crowd. "Mrs. Bryant, Mrs. Bryant!" Bianca yelled as the tears rolled down her face. She tried to catch her breath. "My mom just gave me this letter," Bianca said in between breaths. "I was accepted into the University of Delaware and they're giving me a four year scholarship!"

Mrs. Bryant smiled at Bianca as she hugged her. "That is awesome BJ! You are destined for greatness! You just have to believe that you are!"

Meet the author

Born and raised in Wilmington, Delaware, *Ebony Maddrey* obtained her A.A.S. in Early Childhood Education from Delaware Technical & Community College, her B.S. in Human Services and her M.S. in Community Counseling & Psychology from Springfield College. After teaching for several years, Ebony found the desire to go into counseling. Ebony took a position as an Outpatient Therapist in a mental health clinic that services children and their families in 2006 and has since worked in the field providing individual, family, and group therapy.

Ebony Maddrey has held several positions that include helping and providing services to others. In her quest to educate and motivate young people, Ebony is interchangeably known to her clients as "Ms. Ebony the mom" and "Ms. Ebony the therapist". She has worked as an independent contractor with the C.E.L.E.B. program that continues to provide a form of behavior modification within the Delaware school systems; Ebony has a blog that is published through her own program Flawless

Patchwork, and is also the co-founder of iMlearning, Inc. which is a non-profit organization for young girls.

Ebony has published two books; *The Clinic* and *Let's Talk Families*. She is also a contributing Author in *Diamonds and Pearls*, and is dedicated to producing ongoing materials. Ebony is the mother of three children (Shawn, Jaila, and Bryce) which thus far has been one of her greatest rewards in life. *Garvey* her little spirit and Kaidymar her blossoming butterfly.

www.flawlesspatchwork.com
Email: ebonymaddrey@flawlesspatchwork.com

The Campus

(Excerpt)

It was a bright and sunny day as Bianca walked across campus. "Hey Freshman!" she heard a voice yell from across the yard. Bianca was so focused and determined not to get side tracked by any of the upper classmen. Although, the guy that was yelling at her was extremely cute. He fit what she would describe as an intelligent thug. He was tall and muscular. Had a mesmerizing smile, and donned a certain fraternity label on his red and white jacket. Bianca shot him a smile and a quick wave as she continued to make her way to her afternoon psychology class.

The professor was standing in the doorway as Bianca made her way into the lecture hall. "Good afternoon, my name is Bianca James and I am so excited about taking this course this semester."

"Good afternoon Miss James. I am Dr. Gordon. Welcome to Psych 101, and I am glad that you are eager to learn."

Bianca took her seat in the second to the front row in the large room. She thought to herself, wow, I'm in college sitting in a lecture hall! The other students began to trickle in and fill up each of the fifty plus seats in the class. As Dr. Gordon took his position in front of the class, Bianca turned and noticed the guy from the yard walk into the room. She almost choked when they locked eyes. He flashed those pearly whites and took a seat on the other side of the room. He was positioned in such a way that he was able to stare directly at Bianca.

Oh my God, how am I ever going to get through this semester with this dude that I don't even know making me feel all mushy on the inside? Bianca thought to herself. Her body temperature became elevated as she felt the piercing of his eyes on her. Bianca could feel her hair starting to stick to her neck from sweating profusely.

Bianca tried desperately to focus on what Dr. Gordon was sharing with the class. However, she found it extremely difficult to do so. The cute, nameless guy smiled as he watched her fidgeting in her seat. Damn, Bianca thought, he knows exactly what he's doing.

Bianca had not dated or been with anyone since being with Kenny, her high school crush. She had trust issues and was afraid to allow anyone into her personal space. She made sure to avoid getting to close to anyone who took an interest in her. But there was something different about this guy. She hadn't felt butterflies in a

174

really long time. Bianca couldn't figure out the power of his presence, but she was open to the possibility.

The Clinic

(Excerpt)

"Bianca, girl do you think that you're pregnant?" my sister asked as we compared the dates that our periods usually synchronize.

"Hell no!" I replied and the conversation went on as usual. Four weeks later getting dressed for a night out I realized that my boobs were larger than normal and were somewhat sensitive to the touch. Again, the question was asked, "BJ, girl do you think you're pregnant?" this time coming from my cousin.

"Hell no!" I replied again only this time adding, "I don't even remember the last time that I got it in."

The next morning, just to prove that they were wrong I drove to the Happy Harry's pharmacy to purchase three pregnancy tests. I bought three just in case one was a defect. I had no worries, maybe a little stress from other things but there was no real concern of being pregnant. I paid for my test and went on about my day as usual.

Later that evening I took one of the pregnancy tests before going to bed. Immediately it revealed two pink lines.

"What is this?" I thought as I read over the insert several times. *99% accurate at detecting typical hormone levels from the day of your expected period.* I squinted at the test because one of the lines was fairly faint. As expected this test must be a defect. Therefore, I must fall into that 1% margin of the test not being accurate. Just to be on the safe side, I figured I'd take another test in the morning since people always say that it's best to use your first morning urine to get a more accurate reading.

I hopped in the shower feeling grateful that this would soon be behind me and prepared myself for bed that evening without giving it anymore thought. The next morning, I was up at 5 o'clock in the morning. I opened the second pregnancy test, sat on the toilet, and placed the small white stick into the stream of my first morning urine.

Immediately, two pink lines appeared, one being a little fainter than the other. My mind began to race as I sat there on the toilet staring at the lines on the little white stick.

How in the hell did this happen? This can't be true. This brand must not be effective. I even Googled what the faint line meant on a home pregnancy test from my cell phone as I continued to sit there. I sat there until I could no longer feel my legs.

Tears rolled down my face as my life flashed forward and the previous months surfaced. This is not a good time for me I thought. I have so many goals ahead of me. I'm working towards furthering my career. Oh, God what am I going to do? I said out loud. Then the self-talk began. Ok, get yourself together. You have to call him to let him know what you've just discovered.

As I got up from the toilet I had to brace myself on the sink to keep from falling because my legs felt like they were about to buckle. I washed my face and hands and then took a shower to help me to relax and to reduce the anxiety of making this phone call. I called him when I got out of the shower and of course there was no answer because it was so early in the morning. I hung up and decided to leave a text message. „GM, call me as soon as you get up, " the message read.